Marseille

A Jacques Forêt Mystery

Angela Wren

www.darkstroke.com

Copyright © 2019 by Angela Wren
Photography: Adobe Stock © Lindsay_Helms
Cover Design: Soqoqo
Editor: Stephanie Patterson
All rights reserved.

No part of this book may be used or reproduced in any manner whatsoever without written permission of the author or Crooked Cat except for brief quotations used for promotion or in reviews. This is a work of fiction. Names, characters, and incidents are used fictitiously.

First Dark Edition, darkstroke, Crooked Cat Books. 2019

Discover us online:
www.darkstroke.com

Join us on facebook:
www.facebook.com/groups/darkstroke

Tweet a photo of yourself holding
this book to **@darkstrokedark**
and something nice will happen.

For Maurice and Doris, great friends and travellers through France,
who are still very greatly missed.

Acknowledgments

My very grateful thanks go to :

My local writing colleagues who have patiently listened, commented and encouraged me throughout the writing of this story.

My editor and publisher, without whom none of the books in this series would have been possible, for taking a chance on me way back in 2015.

Readers for selecting my books and reviewers for their most valuable comments.

About the Author

Angela Wren is an actor and director at a small theatre a few miles from where she lives in the county of Yorkshire in the UK. She worked as a project and business change manager – very pressured and very demanding – but she managed to escape, and now she writes books.

She has always loved stories and story-telling, so it seemed a natural progression, to her, to try her hand at writing, starting with short stories. Her first published story was in an anthology, which was put together by the magazine 'Ireland's Own' in 2011.

Angela particularly enjoys the challenge of plotting and planning different genres of work. Her short stories vary between contemporary romance, memoir, mystery, and historical. She also writes comic flash-fiction and has drafted two one-act plays that have been recorded for local radio.

Her full-length stories are set in France, where she likes to spend as much time as possible each year.

Marseille marks the fourth and final story in this quartet of Jacques Forêt mysteries. Angela is moving onto a new writing project. There will be more stories about Jacques in the not too distant future.

Follow Angela at **www.angelawren.co.uk** and **www.jamesetmoi.blogspot.co.uk**.

The Jaques Forêt Mystery series by Angela Wren:

Messandrierre (#1)
Merle (#2)
Montbel (#3)
Marseille (#4)

Marseille

A Jacques Forêt Mystery

samedi

"You wanna be set to run?" He advanced, Colt 45 held out in front. "That what you want, eh?" His victim retreated. Hitting the dusty grey stone of the wall behind, the boy froze.

"Nothing to say, huh?" He took two more steps until they stood toe to toe. Jabbing the barrel of the gun into the youngster's cheek, he pushed his head to the side and held it there, cold hard metal pressuring through skin, into the wall.

"Now, 'ow many bullets yer think I got in 'ere?"

A pair of eyes squinched shut; a whimper, and the small body trembled.

"'Ow many? Could be one, might be six or… What do yer think?" Twisting the pistol further into the soft, smooth flesh, he grinned, raised his chin and let out a roar of laughter. Snapping his attention back to his prey's face, he paused as a well-recognised odour reached his nostrils. He breathed it in. Looking down on the warm straw-coloured pool that was still forming between the child's grey-socked feet, he grimaced.

"Gross, man! That's just gross." He stepped back, gun at arm's length and slowly squeezed the trigger…

september 22nd, 2012

tuesday, september 18th, 2012

Jacques Forêt was finding it hard to concentrate. He shuffled through the papers on his desk without taking in a single word from any of the pages. That morning's board meeting had been a mystery. He had attended in person, but the detail of the business conducted had eluded him. And now, in the early afternoon, he was in his office waiting for the outcome of the management board's private discussion and decision on his proposal to buy-out Vaux Investigations.

As principal investigator and managing director, investigations were his remit and sole responsibility within the family-owned group of businesses. He wanted to be answerable to no one other than himself, and, with some of the money raised from the sale of Beth's property in Leeds and his own savings, he had made the Chairman of the group a very fair offer. At least, that was what he thought he had done.

His initial presentation to the board six months ago had not been well received. The intervening discussions had been acrimonious, and that was down to Mathieu Renaud, the Finance Director. The situation had been exacerbated by Jacques' obsession with a series of police investigations in the surrounding *départements* that were unresolved. Renaud had made numerous references to 'cash-zero work' and the futility of monitoring the 'established legal organisation' at board meetings and at every opportunity in emails to the senior management team. Jacques had developed a passionate dislike for the man.

He picked up a dossier of documents and scanned the name on the front – Richard Laurent Delacroix. He rolled his eyes but flipped open the cover anyway. Attempting to focus his mind, he began to read the uppermost page in an effort to update himself following his month-long leave of absence. Halfway through the second page of notes he tossed it aside, got up, and marched through to the general office where his small team worked.

"I need a distraction," he said slumping down in an empty chair.

Maxim looked up from his daily task of scanning through the print copies of local newspapers, his examination of the online versions already complete.

"There's been very little change since our full update meeting yesterday, Jacques. Didier is out on surveillance for the Éluard matrimonial case. All agreed lines of enquiry on our other cases are being pursued with no new results yet. The latest progress on the Delacroix investigation is already on your desk." He shrugged, a blank look on his pale face.

"Anything, Maxim. Something to stop me trying to second-guess the board's decision about our future." He scrunched his thumb and forefinger across his tired eyes, a deep frown forming on his forehead. When Jacques looked up, his younger colleague was concentrating on something in the paper on his desk. Folding the broadsheet in half and then in half again, Maxim got up.

"This might interest you," he said as he pointed out the relevant article hidden in the bottom right-hand quarter of the page. "It's an update on one of the woodland killings that we've been following for a while." Maxim handed over the journal. "It's the weapon that is of most interest in this case."

Jacques read the first couple of paragraphs under the heading 'No Progress on Hunting Fatality'. His frown deepened as he read the line: '…the recovered bullet is now known to have been fired…'

He looked up.

"From a Derringer? An antique Derringer! How can they be sure about that?"

Maxim puffed his cheeks out as he exhaled. "It doesn't say, but I doubt your ex-colleagues in the police would have released the information to the press if they weren't certain."

"Of course," said Jacques. "So, despite the journalist's nomenclature, it's murder, then, and not a hunting accident. No one goes hunting with a Derringer." He got up and moved across the room to a large display board. A map, with the *département* of Lozère at its centre and the surrounding *départements* of Cantal, Haute-Loire, Ardèche, Gard, and Aveyron, was displayed and spiked with a number of amber coloured pins spread, apparently randomly, across its expanse. He cast his eyes over the map and then fixed his attention on a single pin below the centre.

"Here," he said. "This victim was found here on the Col de St-Pierre on the south side of the D260, which is just on the other side of the boundary with Gard." He pulled out the pin and replaced it with a green one.

"He was fourteen years old," said Maxim joining his boss at the board, a weighty file of papers in his hands. "Found by a *garde-forestier*. It's managed woodland up there, and the body was about two days old when it was discovered." Maxim consulted his notes. "He'd been missing for just over seventeen weeks."

"And that was?"

"May this year when he was snatched, and the body was discovered at the end of the week before last."

Jacques stepped back and scanned the map, trying to recall a detail. "Wasn't there another case about eight or ten months ago with a similar M.O.?"

"Here," said Maxim pointing to another pin, located in a forested area to the north-west in Cantal. "An old Mauser, the C96, was used. A boy again, aged twelve, shot in the back. He'd been missing for over three months, and his body was discovered about a month after he was shot." Maxim paused as he thumbed through his notes.

Jacques' eyes moved systematically across the board. He nodded. "That's two. It's not a pattern…yet. But it is a happenstance that I don't like." In his mind, there was no rhyme or reason to the arrangement of pins in front of him, but there were apparent connections. All the bodies had been found in woodland often used for hunting. The victims had been minors who had disappeared from either home or school without any trace. The newspapers had speculated widely and wildly on the reasons for the youngsters being in the locations where they were found. As far as Jacques was concerned, not one scrap of the speculative column space could be relied upon. But it couldn't be ignored either. Somewhere, in all of those words, was a grain of truth. He would just have to find it. Moving a few steps further back he was able to capture the whole map within his view.

"And that's another connection, Maxim," said Jacques, realisation dawning. "They are all boys. Every one of the victims is male and a minor, apart from Juan de Silva." Jacques nodded towards the pin indicating the pastures just above Messandrierre, a village located some thirty kilometres northeast of his current hometown of Mende. It was a case that was still unresolved.

It was a case that haunted him.

"De Silva?" Maxim hurriedly flicked back through his notes. "Yes, of course, but that was in 2007, and he was killed with a 12-bore shotgun; and he was over sixteen, too."

"Hmm, I remember. But I don't like loose ends and, according to the de Silva family, he had learning difficulties which often made his behaviour mirror someone younger than his age." Pointing at the map again, "And the body found in the ravine on Mont Aigoual the year before last?"

"Boy, thirteen years old, body badly decomposed, some significant damage inflicted by wild animals, and shot with an old Colt 45."

Jacques nodded. "You see, Maxim, there is a pattern forming. You just have to know where to—" He tried to stifle a long and heavy yawn, but failed. "…look." His sentence finally completed, he shook his head. "Excuse me, *mon petit*," he said by way of explanation knowing full well that his colleague didn't need the detail and that he would understand.

Maxim grinned and ran his hand over his close cropped blonde hair. "It does get easier as they grow, but the first three months are the worst," he said. "When Jeannette was born last year I don't think either of us slept more than a—"

Alain Vaux, as Chairman of the board of directors, always commanded immediate attention. A few months short of sixty and dapper in an expensive pale grey suit, white shirt and silver-grey tie that matched his eyes, he appeared in the doorway and marched in.

With a simple nod to Jacques, he said, "If you've got a few moments, I'd like a word please." And Vaux stepped back out of the room.

Jacques looked at Maxim, hoping his own internal worry was not evident on his face. He'd been waiting for this moment since he came back into the office early the previous morning.

"I'll get us the best deal I can." He looked Maxim in the eye. After a few seconds, Maxim nodded, and Jacques saw the beginnings of a weak but resigned smile move over his colleague's face. "I'll see what Alain has to say," he said as he moved swiftly across the room to the door. "In the meantime can you set out, in a tabular form, all the details we have for each of the incidents on the map, please? I want ages, names, dates, weapons and locations and any other detail that you think is appropriate."

Closing the door behind him, Jacques paused for a moment, took a deep breath and ran his hands through his hair. He marched the length of the corridor to his own office.

"Alain, sorry to keep you waiting. I'm guessing you are here to convey the board's decision," he said as he took his place at his desk.

Alain relaxed back into the chair opposite and straightened his tie. "I'll be direct with you, Jacques. The board have not yet made a decision, but we are close. Had we taken a vote today, your proposal for the buy-out would have been refused by a majority of one."

Mathieu Renaud, thought Jacques. He waited for Alain to

continue, deciding to say nothing for the moment.

"So, the decision isn't final yet, but…" Alain stood and moved over to the floor-to-ceiling windows. "It's not final because Mathieu wants to go over the figures again, and I wanted to ask you, one last time, if there was any possibility that you might withdraw the proposal." Alain turned to face him, hands in his trouser pockets, demeanour giving nothing away.

Jacques shook his head. "Alain, I greatly appreciate your support, and I know how much this business area means to you personally, but I want to be my own boss. I realise, from what you've just said, that my proposal has split the board and I can understand how difficult some of the discussions you've had over the last few months must have been. But, here at Vaux, I have a board of directors to answer to all the time. You've seen all the comments from Mathieu about my interest in a spate of child killings. Mathieu thinks everything comes down to euros and *centimes*. It doesn't. There's more to this work. Sometimes it's just about collecting information. Just like police work, private investigation is always reliant on information. I'm a policeman at heart, Alain. Always have been and always will be. And as such, my only master is the law. Perhaps I made a mistake in leaving the *gendarmerie*, but I know I did not make a mistake in coming here. I have revolutionised how we operate. I have a dedicated and hard-working team who bring in results from which only the corporate organisation benefits. I want us to survive by our own efforts, Alain. I want us to be answerable only to our clients and ourselves with the backing of the law." Jacques set his jaw and waited for what he expected to be yet more pressure to comply.

Alain moved back across the room and shoved the chair opposite Jacques out of the way, allowing him space to perch on the corner of the desk.

"I can see how determined you are, Jacques, and I respect that. I also acknowledge the income you've brought into this organisation. I agree you and your team do not benefit directly, but you do indirectly." He glanced around the room. "The space you occupy, the technical support, the—"

"I am well aware of that." Jacques dropped his gaze to the desk. His response had been a little more forceful and his tone sharper than he had intended. A few seconds later, looking directly at Alain, he leaned forward, fingers tightly interlocked as he rested his hands and forearms on his desk.

"I am only too well aware and grateful for that. And my proposal sets out three options, remaining here and paying the going rate, remaining here and creating a specially tailored and independent agreement for space and / or services provided, or moving to a completely different location. And for the first two options, I believe the figures suggested are very fair and equitable. If the only sticking point is the money, then let's talk numbers. Get Mathieu in here and let's crash the numbers. Right here. Right now." Damn that man, Renaud, he thought. *You're behind all of this!*

Alain shook his head and stood. "It's not the numbers, Jacques. Although there are a few errors that Mathieu has spotted that he wants to cross-check, that's all."

Jacques frowned, pushed his chair out from his desk and slumped back.

"I'm the sticking point, Jacques. In the three years you've been here, you've transformed this area of business. A business that I first began when I joined the group because of my father's failing health. Over the last year, you've won over most of the board members with your practical and level-headed input at board meetings. You've even won over Mathieu, and that's no easy task. If you want the brutal truth, I'm the sticking point, Jacques, because I think there is still a lot that we can learn from you and, frankly, I don't want to see you leave."

As Jacques absorbed the enormity of Alain's statement, he became aware of the gradually increasing noise of some commotion nearby. Trusting that Maxim would deal with the matter, Jacques was about to respond when the door of his office flew open.

Marie Mancelle, a neighbour from Messandrierre, burst in, tears streaming down her face. Her daughter, Célestine, was wailing and following on behind, with Maxim bringing up the rear.

"Marie?"

"It's Pierre," she bawled. "He's gone, Jacques! He's been taken."

Alain nodded to Jacques, "I'll leave you to deal with this," he said as he strode to the door. "We'll talk again later in the week." He slipped from the room.

Jacques was on his feet, his arm around Marie's shoulders as he shepherded her to the chair that Alain had recently vacated.

"It's alright," said Jacques as Maxim dithered in the doorway. "I'll handle this if you would make some tea please, with lemon and plenty of sugar. Can you also let the *police municipale* know that we think a child may be in danger? And when you come back with the tea, it would be helpful if you could stay and take notes."

"Someone's taken Pierre," wailed Marie. "He's not answering his phone. It's dead. He's gone, Jacques." Marie collapsed into a fit of sobs, distressing her daughter who began to mewl, fear and confusion in her eyes.

tuesday, september 18th, 16.54

Settled with the tea, Jacques waited for Marie to calm down sufficiently to take a couple of sips. Her adopted daughter, Célestine, wouldn't leave her side, and Jacques understood why. In her short life thus far, the seven-year-old had found the world of adults bewildering and cruel. Her painful past meant that knowing who to trust and when would be a constant and fearful dilemma that would dominate her childhood. In the future, as an adolescent, her past would be an ever-present dark and threatening shadow, and as an adult knowing where to safely seek assurance and reliance would be a large grey cloud that would colour her every thought, word, and action for the rest of her life.

While she recognised and knew Jacques, she was still reticent to talk to him unless her older brother, Marie's natural son Pierre, was there.

"Marie, I know how hard this is for you, but you need to take me through what has happened. Step by step, alright?" He continued to hold her hands in his until she nodded her understanding. "Have some more tea," he encouraged as he grabbed his notebook and pen from the desk.

Marie, still trembling, reached for the drink. Holding the cup in both hands, she gulped the warm, sweet liquid and stared at the floor. Célestine mithered at her mother's knee.

Jacques smiled at the child. "It's all right, *ma petite*, you and *maman* are both safe."

Célestine moved even closer to her mother who sniffed and swept her hanky under her eyes. "It's Monsieur Jacques," Marie said and put her arm around her daughter. "You know Monsieur Jacques. You carried flowers for him and Madame Elizabeth in church, *ma chérie*, remember?"

The child looked up at her mother and nodded.

Aware of the need to act quickly, Jacques checked his

watch. "Maxim has telephoned the police, and they should be on their way. They have set procedures to follow, Marie, and we need to get down as much as we can, as clearly as we can, to help them."

Marie nodded as she tried to control a fresh wave of tears. "I know," she said. She took a deep breath and wiped her hands across her face. "I was to pick up both children from school in Badaroux, just over twenty minutes ago. When I arrived, neither of them were waiting in the playground. I thought they might be with one of their teachers in the classroom, so I left the car and went in." She looked up at Jacques, her face crumbling into tears again.

"Marie, just think back carefully and tell me what happened next?"

"I went in, and Célestine was waiting in the entrance hall with Pierre's teacher, Madame Piquet." She dabbed her cheeks. "I asked where Pierre was, but the teacher said he was in the playground. I told her he wasn't and asked her again where he had gone."

"Just a moment. You didn't see Pierre in the playground when you arrived, but Célestine was with the teacher inside."

Marie nodded.

Jacques continued. "Where do the children normally meet after class?"

"They wait for each other in the entrance hall and then come out into the playground to wait for me unless it's raining."

Jacques glanced at the child. Her eyes were red and swollen, her expression glum. She looked away. He turned his attention to her mother.

"Did Madame Piquet say anything else?"

"Only that today Pierre did things differently. They both went outside and then a few moments later Pierre came back with his sister and left her. He told Madame Piquet he would be back in a minute. I..." Marie looked around and pulled her daughter towards her. "I don't know why he did that." Resting her arm on the corner of the desk, she pulled her fingers backwards and forwards over her forehead. "I don't know why he did that," she whispered.

Jacques recognised the look of utter helplessness on her face. And in that moment his previous police training failed him as he swallowed back his fear for what might have happened to Pierre. He cleared his throat and shifted in his chair.

"Alright... Umm, let's move onto something else. What was Pierre wearing today?"

Marie frowned, "Umm, his favourite red and grey trainers, his grey jeans, a red polo shirt, grey socks, I think. Yes, I noticed he had put on odd socks when he first came down to breakfast, and I made him change them. He took his favourite hoodie, too. The black one with the white blaze across the back."

Jacques looked across at Maxim who had been sitting silently at the back of the room. "We will need to pass on that information to the police and get it circulated to all our missing persons websites and social media pages. Can you type up the description and deal with that, please?"

Maxim nodded and darted out of the room.

"Good," said Jacques. "And what about his father or grandfather? Could he be with either of them?"

Marie shook her head. "No, Martin is in Lyon with the opera company, and his grandfather has been here in Mende all day, at the *préfecture*. And if he had decided to go to either of them, I would have known. Pierre would have told me."

"OK, what about friends? Are there any friends that he might have gone to see?"

"No," said Marie, shaking her head. "No. He would never do that without telling me first, and I've had no messages or calls from him today."

Jacques noticed that Célestine was tugging at her mother's jacket sleeve, with a questioning look on her face. He smiled at the little girl and squatted down on one knee in front of her. "Has *maman* got that wrong, Célestine?"

Glancing from Jacques to Marie and then back again, the

child nodded.

Jacques set his face as his thoughts moved into murky waters. *If he did meet someone, who was it and what kind of friend? Would someone as young as you really know?* He sighed. *There's so much about your past that I don't know too. How to proceed?*

Frowning, he shifted to his other knee to give himself a moment to collect his thoughts. Then, Jacques decided on some simple, straightforward questioning.

"Did Pierre meet a friend today?"

Another nod.

"And this was after school, Célestine?"

The door of Jacques' office opened quietly, and Maxim held it wide to admit Investigating Magistrate Bruno Pelletier. Jacques nodded to Maxim and placed a finger against his lips as Bruno slipped into the room and took the chair at the back. Jacques repeated his question, and Célestine cast another questioning glance at her mother.

"It's alright, *chérie*. Pierre isn't in trouble. If he did meet a friend, then we need to know who, so that we can find him." She pulled her daughter closer. The child nodded again.

Jacques cast Bruno a glance. He quickly noted down the name of the school on a blank page ripped from his notebook, added the abbreviation 'CCTV', and handed it to the magistrate. Pelletier took it and moved silently out of the room.

"Do you know the name of Pierre's friend?"

Célestine shook her head, her eyes wide she clutched at her mother's arm.

Jacques was on the point of asking about her apparent dislike of the friend when he decided he needed to clarify something else first.

"Is this friend a boy?"

"Yes, but I don't like him. He shouts," Célestine whispered, still clinging on to Marie.

"Would you know him if you saw him again?"

The child nodded. Jacques smiled at her. "Thank you.

You're very brave, and you've been very helpful."

Jacques stood and took a deep breath. *I have to stay focussed.* "We must let the police handle this now, Marie. If I question her any further, it could compromise any possible court case, when it comes to that. Magistrate Pelletier is here, and you must speak with him. An appropriate and experienced officer will need to be assigned to the case to question Célestine further."

Marie sighed but nodded her assent. "But you will be there, won't you?"

"I will do everything I can to help, but we must follow the appropriate procedure." Jacques maintained his calm and composed approach in front of Marie. Inside, his gut was churning. *The first twenty-four hours are critical.* He reminded himself that he needed to take this case a step at a time.

Some hours later, Marie and her daughter were safely in the care of a female officer who had escorted them back to their home in Messandrierre. Bruno and Jacques were alone in the magistrate's office in Mende.

"There's little more that we can do tonight, Jacques, so tell me what you know about the family." Bruno pulled the open window too and settled himself back behind his large untidy desk.

"They're a very close family, I think. Martin is frequently away from home, which is why Pierre has had his own phone for a while now. He can keep in touch with his *papa* whenever he is on tour with the opera company. When the company are resident in Marseille, Martin lives in their apartment near the old port but comes home to Messandrierre one or two weekends a month and sometimes during the week, depending on his performances."

"Ah, the husband is away a lot, the wife alone in the village. Would you say the marriage is a happy one?"

Taken aback by the question, Jacques let out a long slow breath. "Who really knows what goes on inside a marriage, Bruno?" He shrugged. "To me, they have always seemed very happy and, as far as I'm aware, there's no gossip in the village about either of the parents."

"I see. And the little girl?"

"Adopted and benefiting from life with the Mancelle family. And isn't that a testament to the stability within the household? The fact that the authorities trust them to adopt a child with emotional difficulties?"

Jacques sat back in his chair and rested his left ankle on his right knee waiting for Bruno to respond, but the magistrate took out his handkerchief and began to polish his spectacles.

"The child is still withdrawn," continued Jacques. "But not as much as when she first came to live with them last year. And Pierre, from what I have seen, has a great deal to do with that. He dotes on her, and he has become very protective of her."

"I see." The magistrate put on his spectacles as he rose from his desk. "Come with me. There's something that doesn't quite add up in my mind, Jacques."

Getting up, Jacques followed Pelletier out into the corridor and then into a substantial incident room. At one end was a large board with a map covered with pins. Jacques studied the display. His eyes traced the lines of thin red twine to the notes and photos around the edge. The map bore a striking resemblance to the one he had in his suite of offices.

"This boy here, killed with a Derringer on the Col de St-Pierre, was estranged from his father and unsettled with his mother and her relatively new partner." Pelletier pointed to another pin and the linking picture. "This boy killed with a Mauser in neighbouring Cantal was unruly at school. His father left when the child was six. And this boy killed with the Colt 45 and found on Mont Aigoual had a father who was mostly drunk, known to take drugs, and had been unemployed for over ten years. At this particular boy's school, the teachers were concerned because they identified signs of possible physical abuse. If we now look at this—"

"Pierre and his family don't fit the established profile for all the other kidnappings and subsequent killings. That's what you're saying, isn't it?"

"I'm just raising the question, Jacques."

"Have you established any connection between the boys yet?" He moved to his left and sat on the edge of a nearby empty desk.

Bruno shook his head. "Not one that will work for all of them. The investigation team are still looking. But there are some details that have not been released to the press. The boy found in the ravine on Mont Aigoual had small traces of drugs on his clothes."

"So, he could have been a runner for his father." Jacques looked at the map and shook his head as he realised that he didn't want to verbalise his next thought. "Or he could have been a user himself. How does that happen, Bruno? How does a thirteen-year-old get hold of drugs?"

Bruno raised his eyebrows. "I know, Jacques. It's tragic. But it happens very easily, these days. Perhaps the more important question is, what has happened in this boy's life to make him believe that drugs are any form of an answer?"

"Yes, you're right. Somehow, in moving to this area, I thought I could leave the soullessness of the drug culture behind me in Paris."

Bruno shrugged. "Ah, perhaps a few years ago. But not anymore."

"Thinking about Pierre, his family background, I'm finding it very difficult to accept that there is a drugs connection. Pierre is too sensible."

"But he's only nine years old and therefore vulnerable. We're still gathering evidence about connections between these boys, and I don't want to eliminate anything from our enquiries until I'm sure."

Jacques studied his ex-colleague's face. There was a trace of sadness in his eyes. For the boys, Jacques reasoned as he thought about the problematic existence each of the youngsters might have endured in the days and weeks leading up to their respective deaths.

Pierre, I hope you're safe. His thoughts then turned to his new son, and he wondered how he would keep him safe from the modern world.

An officer from a desk at the opposite end of the incident room approached Bruno.

"We've got confirmation from Lyon. Monsieur Martin Mancelle, the boy's father, has not heard from him since yesterday morning before his son left for school. Monsieur Mancelle is on stage at the moment, but he will be returning to Mende first thing in the morning. He's not certain he will be able to get here in time for the planned press announcement, though."

"Thanks," said Bruno as the officer returned to his desk. "Can you make the press conference if Marie needs someone to support her?"

"Of course."

Bruno looked at his watch. "It's getting late, and you need to go home to your own family."

Jacques grinned and nodded. "I've missed them these past two days while I've been back at the office, but I'm not missing the lack of sleep."

Bruno smiled benignly. "You'll get used to it," he said as they walked back to his office. "And when he's a teenager, it's an entirely different sort of worry and sleeplessness."

Ignoring the last remark, Jacques collected his things together. "Pierre's a clever boy, Bruno, and his ambition to be a policeman is still a current one. If he can let us know where he is or what has happened, I'm sure he'll find a way."

"I hope so. We both know what the possibilities are for him if we don't find him quickly."

A cloud descended in Jacques' mind when he left the room. He ran down the stairs to the entrance, his thoughts focussed on the map. His gut tightened. *Is that Pierre's fate?* Out on the street, he stopped and took several deep breaths. Heartfelt emotion was pricking at the back of his eyes.

I can't let that happen.

"I won't let that happen," he said, pinching the bridge of his nose tightly.

tuesday, september 18th, 22.06

Jacques carefully laid his bunch of keys in the dish on the vestibule table of his apartment in Mende. Walking into the living space he found his sister, Thérèse, reading. She shushed him as soon as she looked up. Jacques sank down on the sofa beside her.

"How's Beth?" he whispered.

"Exhausted. She's asleep in your room and Lucien is here," she said indicating the small carrycot on the floor beside the sofa. "Don't disturb him, please."

"OK." Jacques slid off the sofa and crawled over to his son. "Hello, *mon petit*, and how are you this evening?" He gently glazed his little finger across the cheek of the tiny sleeping face. "And now you are four weeks, three days and…" he glanced at his watch, 22.09, "nine minutes old, did you know that?"

Thérèse smiled at her younger brother. "Carry on like that and when he's older, he'll have you wrapped around his little finger!"

"Too late," he said. "He already has."

Lucien stirred in his sleep, but didn't wake. Jacques stood, threw off his jacket and sat down. He felt all-in and guessed that he probably looked it too.

"You're very late, Jacques. Beth is still fragile and she was worried about you. It took me almost an hour to convince her to go and lie down and get some rest." His sister marked her page and put the book on the coffee table.

"It's not been a good day. The board are still not happy with my buy-out proposal and Pierre Mancelle, the grandson of the *Maire* in Messandrierre, is missing. A possible abduction. His mother, Marie, is quite understandably distraught. You met them last year at the wedding."

"Yes, I remember. Such a lovely boy. Who would do something like that?"

Jacques pulled his weary bones off the sofa and grimaced at his sister. The map in the office sprang to mind and he cast his fears for Pierre to the very furthest recesses of his conscious thoughts.

"Unfortunately, the world isn't full of honest and trustworthy people such as ourselves," he said as he dragged himself to the kitchen.

Thérèse checked on the child before getting up to follow him. "Is he in much danger?"

Jacques paused, his hand on the handle of the fridge door. *What do I say to that?* Head down, he let his eyes wander across the random markings on the tiles on the floor as he considered his options. *She might be a mother but she's not the victim's mother*. He turned to look at her. *I need to be honest*.

"Please don't repeat what I'm about to say to anyone. Pierre could be in very grave danger. If he's with a friend, which I very much doubt, we should be able to find him quickly, and he will be safe. If he has been abducted, as we firmly suspect, he could be dead already. If not, he may well be very soon. My team at Vaux have done everything they can. We have his picture, a detailed description and a list of the clothing he was wearing posted on all the regular social media sites and websites that we use to trace people. The police, of course, are following their own appropriate procedures. Now, we wait. We wait and we follow up every possible lead."

Thérèse let a tear role down her face. "I see."

Jacques turned his attention to the contents of the fridge as he willed his mind not to consider the possibilities for Pierre. *I need a very clear head for this one.* Moving jars around the shelf and opening drawers Jacques sought to distract himself.

"I made some tomato and basil soup for Beth." Thérèse

wiped a second tear from her cheek, an emotional tremor still evident in her voice. "There's plenty left if you want some. She hardly ate anything again today. I'm very worried about her, Jacques."

"Yes, so am I." The change of subject welcome, he pulled out the container of soup, poured some into a bowl and slotted it into the microwave. "But she won't go and see her doctor." He punched in the required time.

"Then make her go and see him or bring the doctor here to her."

Jacques looked at the set expression on his sister's face. It was the same one she'd used when they were at the *lycée* in Paris together when she'd told him that the girl he was interested in had been deliberately avoiding him and that he should forget her and move on. And it was the same look she'd given him when he'd returned to his parent's apartment in Paris because his mother was dying, only to find that he was too late.

The microwave pinged. He reached in for his soup, collected a spoon from one of the drawers, and moved across to the dining table. Thérèse brought some bread and the cutting board and followed him.

After two or three mouthfuls, he ignored the knife and ripped a piece of bread from the remains of the *pain* and dunked it in his soup.

"So, I'm not imagining Beth's odd behaviour if you've seen it too."

Thérèse frowned, "I think she needs help. Professional help. I know I've only been here since last week, but… There are things that I recognise. Do you remember how I was just after our eldest was born?"

Jacques nodded and helped himself to some more bread.

"The lack of appetite, constantly worrying about Lucien despite re-assurances that everything is alright, her lack of understanding of time, the constant tiredness and her French. I don't understand. It's as though, suddenly, she has forgotten all of her French."

"We both agreed, some months ago, that we wanted

Lucien to be bi-lingual and that we would use both languages." Jacques scraped his spoon around the side of his bowl.

"Yes, I can see the sense of that, but, I said something to her earlier this afternoon and I could see in her face that she was desperately trying to recall the words to respond. I think she needs some professional help, Jacques, and she needs you."

Jacques stared at her. *And there it is again, that look and so like maman's, too.* It was only then that it struck him that he hadn't really noticed before just how much his sister resembled their mother. Her dark hair beginning to grey at the front, her bright blue eyes, and that piercing stare fixed on him.

When did that happen? When did you suddenly become so like maman?

"Jacquomo," she placed her hand on his forearm. "I'm not qualified to give you a diagnosis, only a doctor can do that. But I am worried and I don't want Beth to suffer unnecessarily if there is a simple and easy solution. But there is something wrong. Even I can see that there's something wrong. She needs help."

He winced at her use of his pet name within the family. Even Beth didn't know about that. "You haven't called me that since we were teenagers together."

"No, but you always used to listen when I did."

Lucien shifted under his coverlet and let out a little gurgle. Thérèse got up, collected the carrycot and brought it across to where she had been sitting and placed it on the seat.

"Your son needs your attention," she said lifting the baby out and giving him to Jacques.

"Hello, little one," he said using English as he cradled the child in his arms.

Thérèse nodded and smiled. "I'll warm some milk and you can feed him."

Jacques nodded automatically. He wasn't listening. He was engrossed with the new being that had come into his life just over a month ago, who was now gazing up at him.

"I think *papa* will be sleeping in your room tonight," he said. "*Maman* is very, very tired." Lucien let out a little squeal. Jacques smiled as he thought about how uncomfortable the small sofa bed was in the room that they now referred to as the nursery. I'll cope, he thought. *Even after the day I've had today*. But he knew he wouldn't sleep. He would be listening for every sound from his son's cot, his investigator's mind would be consumed by Pierre, and his personal worries would be all about Beth.

wednesday, september 19th, 05.38

Sleep had mostly evaded Jacques. At the dining room table, a lukewarm black coffee in a breakfast cup on his right and a plate with a half-eaten slice of toasted yesterday's bread and jam on his left, Jacques was reading information on the screen on his laptop. He scrolled back to the top of the document. Grabbing the toast, he munched through it and washed it down with the dregs from the coffee cup. He started reading again.

"Lucien!" Beth ran in from the bedroom. "Where's Lucien?"

Jacques jumped to his feet and moved across to her. "He's here with me." He took her hand and gently led her across to the table. Lifting the carrycot onto the chair he'd been sitting in, he whispered, "Look! Lucien is here. He's asleep."

A relieved smile spread across Beth's face as she focussed on her son.

"There you are," she said as she lifted the carrycot. "There you are." With the cot on the sofa beside her, she gently re-arranged the coverlet around the sleeping child. "I need to know where he is at all times, Jacques."

Beth looked at him for the first time. The beatific smile reserved for their son had morphed into an accusatory stare. Her eyes were steady but hooded and the distance that had developed between them over the last couple of months stretched into a chasm.

"I've fed him and changed him."

"You should've woken me." She physically turned herself away.

"You needed the rest, Beth." He moved across to the sofa so that he was facing her. Her only interest was the child, to whom she was softly humming.

"He's my son, too." There was no response. "Beth?" The low humming continued and after a moment or two Jacques strode through to their bedroom. He needed a shower and a change of clothes. The ones he stood up in were from the previous day and when he had eventually fallen into a fitful sleep they had become his night time attire.

wednesday, september 19th, 09.52

The flashes from the cameras were thick and constant as Magistrate Pelletier and Monsieur and Madame Mancelle took their places at the top table for the press conference. Pelletier waited for the initial hubbub to die down.

"*Mesdames et Messieurs*," he began his right hand open and held up to quell the last of the talk amongst the journalists. "There have been a number of boys who have been abducted in our neighbouring *départements*. Today, I am very sorry to have to tell you that one of our own boys is missing. He's nine years old and from the village of Messandrierre just north of here. His name is Pierre Mancelle. It appears that he was taken from outside his school in nearby Badaroux yesterday afternoon. A recent picture and a detailed description of the clothing he was wearing have been circulated to you all already." Pelletier glanced at his notes.

"Missing or abducted, Magistrate Pelletier? Which is it?" A local journalist at the back of the room took advantage of the slight pause.

Pelletier acknowledged the question with the slightest of nods and resumed his prepared address. "At the end of the school day, yesterday, Pierre and his younger sister were waiting to be collected in the playground. We have CCTV footage that clearly shows that someone, off camera, attracts Pierre's attention. At first he takes a few steps forward, but then hesitates and returns to where his sister is waiting. They both go back into school. A few moments later Pierre re-appears in the playground and walks towards the gate. He is walking purposefully. Perhaps towards someone he knows or recognises. We are talking to his close friends and classmates. But, it was the end of the school day, there was a lot of commotion as parents, grandparents, and other relatives and friends came to collect the children." Pelletier looked up and fixed his eyes on the room. "Someone else was there yesterday. Someone who had a different motive for being there. We want to know who that person was. A parent, a child, a friend must have seen something and we are asking for anyone who might have information, who might have seen something unusual, to come forward. An incident room has been set up and officers are waiting to take calls. Any information, no matter how insignificant, may be of great importance to us. Please, if you were there at the school, yesterday, get in touch with us. A child's life is at stake."

At the last sentence, Marie finally lost her fragile composure and broke down in tears. Martin tried to comfort her as the journalists started throwing out questions to the magistrate and the parents.

Pelletier silenced them by standing and stating, "No questions at this point."

A female officer came to Marie's side and along with Martin guided her away from the table and out of the room. Pelletier followed on.

At the back of the public area, Jacques had been watching and listening. He waited until Marie and Martin were safely out of the way and in the restricted part before making a move. As he reached the doorway, the journalist who had interrupted Pelletier stopped him.

"Jacques Forêt, isn't it?"

Jacques stepped to one side to let the remaining attendees go ahead of him.

"Previously *inspecteur principal* for the Paris police, wasn't it?" The journalist stretched his arm across the doorway to block it and grinned.

Jacques took another step back and waited in silence.

"Are the *police municipale* employing failed detectives from Paris now?"

The insolent smile on the journalist's face and the tone of

his voice were deliberately meant to goad. Jacques knew that and refused to let himself be drawn.

"Let me pass, please?" He maintained his composure.

"Come on, Monsieur Forêt." The journalist edged closer and lowered his voice. "What's your role in this?"

Jacques slipped through the doorway without responding and strode down the corridor, the journalist in pursuit.

"Monsieur Forêt? There's a story here; I can smell it. What are you doing here?"

Jacques kept walking.

"Is it drugs, Monsieur?" The journalist quickened his pace and came up beside his quarry. "That was your last case in Paris, wasn't it?"

Jacques stopped dead in his tracks. He looked the man straight in the eye. "I have nothing to add to Magistrate Pelletier's statement," he said, maintaining his stare, his voice steady but quiet.

"So, there is something here." A wry smile spread across the journalist's face.

"No comment," said Jacques through clenched teeth as he strode on, his pace doubled by his anger. At the desk at the public entrance to the station, Jacques showed his card to the officer on duty.

"Jacques Forêt to see Bruno Pelletier," he said. The officer nodded and released the lock on the door leading through to the area for authorised personnel only. Reaching the stairs, Jacques ascended two at a time and disappeared into Pelletier's office knowing that the journalist could not catch up with him again, no matter what strategies he employed with the desk officer.

"That went well," said Jacques as he closed the door behind him.

"Let's hope it gets us some corroboration for Célestine's statement and a more detailed description of the person who was waiting for Pierre which we can then circulate."

The magistrate removed his rimless spectacles and began to polish them with his handkerchief.

"And the CCTV footage?"

"In the incident room and you're welcome to view it. If you spot anything that you think we may have missed, let me know immediately."

Jacques nodded, crossed the hallway and disappeared into another room.

wednesday, september 19th, 10.14

On a busy street in the northern city of Rouen, a tall muscled man with bright blue eyes sat in an office listening to the final instructions from the *notaire*.

"Some signatures, Monsieur Vauquelin, and then I can hand over the keys," said the lawyer as he presented some papers, the places to sign marked in pencil, and offered his pen. Guy Vauquelin pulled his own biro from the inside pocket of his jacket. He only glanced at the documents; he really had no need to do any more as he was used to dealing with this kind of paperwork. He signed as requested.

A few moments later, he was shaking hands with the lawyer and being escorted out of the building. A smug smile on his face, Guy Vauquelin walked away from the office block and towards the street where his hire car was parked. *Couldn't have gone better.* He patted the pocket of his jacket, making sure that he could feel the hard outline shapes of the keys as confirmation that they were really there.

"Could not have gone better," he muttered to himself as he turned down a side street and caught his unfamiliar reflection in a shop window. Pausing momentarily he grinned at his alter ego and strode on. It was a fifteen-minute walk to Saint-Sever on the other side of the river and he could have taken the tram, but he wanted to preserve his anonymity as much as possible. He also wanted to ensure that he wasn't being tailed and to leave no obvious indication of the direction from which he had come into the city. After all, he had reasoned when planning this particular piece of work, it was easy to be lost or not remembered in a city of around a half a million residents that was still swelled by foreign visitors. He took a right and crossed the Seine, narrowly avoiding a collision on the bridge with a group of Japanese tourists interested only in posing for photos. He summoned his perfect Paris-French and apologised.

"And if the villagers in Messandrierre could've heard that…" he muttered to stifle his own rueful laugh. A smile in his eyes, he noticed that he had caught the attention of a young woman passing in the opposite direction. He nodded and wished her a good day as though she were a neighbour. *And this time next week, if anyone bothers to ask, she won't even be able to recall what I look like.* A wistfulness came over him as he wondered about her. *Shame, she might have been fun.*

He quickened his pace and didn't look back. The car he had hired was parked in the shade of the plane trees on the quay, just a few metres away. As he approached, he punched the fob for the vehicle and moved straight to the back. Another button on the fob and the boot sprang open. Retrieving a small holdall, he closed the boot, moved to the passenger door and dumped the bag on the seat. Getting behind the wheel he set the satellite navigation to take him to *place* Bernard Tissot. Indicating, he joined the heavy, mid-morning traffic as soon as he was able. The drive to the station compound was short but slow. He parked in a designated spot and dropped off the keys.

From there he entered the station and made straight for the gents. Not that he would be catching a train. That would be too simple and too easy to trace. In a cubicle, he retrieved a small mirror from his bag and an electric razor. He deftly razored away his five days' growth of stubble and grinned at his clean reflection. Next, he took out some clothes and hung them on the hook on the back of the door and began to change. With everything packed into a second, differently coloured canvas bag, he collapsed his holdall and packed that in the bag, too. Emerging from the cubicle, he checked his appearance in the mirror above the wash-hand basins. As a final flourish, he donned his black fedora and pulled it low.

His transformation complete, he left, walked to a nearby apartment block where he had temporarily rented a small place with parking for his own car in an underground car park. He keyed in the barrier code and went straight to his vehicle. Opening the boot, he slung in the bag and slammed it shut. In his comfortable driver's seat, hat removed, he checked his rear-view mirror and grinned.

"It may have been Guy Vauquelin who went into the station," he said to his reflection. "But it was Richard Laurent Delacroix who came out." He winked at himself, started the engine and, shifted into first gear. There was very little that was true about Richard Laurent Delacroix. Not least his name, and it caused him no concern.

About forty-five minutes later, Delacroix was driving through the centre of Verdon-le-Grand, a small town some thirty kilometres south east of Rouen. According to his satellite navigation device, the street he wanted was a few hundred metres ahead on his right. He slowed for the traffic and kept looking right. *And that's it.* A smile of recognition passed across his face as he momentarily contemplated the white iron fencing around the enclosed garden of the hotel on the corner. *That's the place.* The car indicator blinking in his peripheral vision, he waited and took the right turn as soon as a gap in the traffic allowed, then travelled down the street slowly looking for number 38.

"And there it is," he said to himself as he drew up outside a small, old and uncared for property. He killed the engine and sat there for a few moments. There was no garden. The front door, with windows on either side of it, opened directly onto the quiet street beneath a long low roof with two old-fashioned dormer windows inset.

"Small," he said to himself. "Usefully small."

He got out and locked the vehicle. Retrieving the keys from his jacket, he checked the labels and found the one that fitted the front door. The lock was stiff but he managed to shift it and pushed at the heavy wooden door. The lintel was low and he had to duck to walk through. Inside, the place was full of dust and smelt of age and decay. He let his eyes adjust to the lack of light and wished he had remembered to collect his torch from the boot of the car. Moving slowly, he carefully walked through the rooms. Behind the house was a small yard with what appeared to be an equally small outhouse.

Perfect. Absolutely perfect.

Climbing the narrow stairs, he checked the roof space. The smell of damp and fustiness was even stronger. Looking up, he saw the source of the problem. A couple of the ridge tiles had been dislodged and the weather had done the rest. *Need to get that fixed and watertight urgently.*

Retracing his steps, he made a decision. He'd have a late lunch at the hotel on the main street, book a room for a couple of nights and then come back to the house in more suitable clothing and have a proper look around. The seven-hour drive back to Messandrierre could wait until another day.

Emerging into the sunshine again, he stood on the street and looked up and down. It was as quiet as the last time he had visited some six months previously. He glanced at the newer properties on the other side of the road, all with their windows hung behind with net curtains of various colours and patterns. He grinned to himself and turned to lock the door unaware of the enormity that those few seconds would assume in the coming days.

***

At number 37 *rue des Déportés Martyrs*, eighty-two year old Monsieur Archambault Hervé, the long-time occupant of the property, drew aside the net curtain that his daughter-in-law had recently laundered for a moment and then let it drop. From his comfortable and well-worn armchair behind the window gauze, Monsieur Hervé watched as the man at number 38 returned to his car, got in and, after fastening his seatbelt, set off and drove further down the road. Monsieur

Hervé waited patiently. He thought the man might be using the entrance to another property further down the street to turn around. The post van and delivery drivers always used it as did many of the other residents. A few moments later his patience was rewarded and the vehicle returned. As it passed his house, Monsieur Hervé noted down the registration in a small well-thumbed notebook.

wednesday, september 19th, 11.44

Following the press conference, Jacques had been viewing CCTV footage all morning. His only interruption was the call from Beth's physician offering an appointment later that day. Having discussed it with Beth and his sister over the telephone, they agreed that he would meet them at the surgery just before the appointment. His concentration broken, his mind spiralled into a sea of worry. *Was it just the baby blues or something more serious?* His searches on the internet the previous evening and early that morning had been confusing. The symptoms, the causes, the treatment, the possible diagnoses, had just presented him with more questions than answers and a greater level of worry. He wished he'd not undertaken the research.

He checked his watch, 11.48. *I need to focus.* He looked back at the monitor and moved the footage back a couple of minutes to make sure he hadn't missed anything important whilst his thoughts had been elsewhere.

Jacques stared at the screen and the paused CCTV footage. In one corner there was something unusual. Something different. He zoomed in on the item that had caught his attention and tried to make sense of what he was seeing. *A car tyre?*

"Can't be; it looks too small," he muttered to himself.

He advanced the footage slowly and kept his eye on the same corner of the screen. The object disappeared and shortly afterwards was replaced by something similar. *A second car tyre?* He zoomed out a little, reversed the footage and played it again slowly. At the third re-run he grabbed his notebook, a look of satisfaction on his face.

"It's a scooter," he said as he jotted down a possible manufacturer's name and drew a heavy circle around it. Then he checked the screen again and noted down the time and date, '13.48.12, 17/09/2012'. He added the word '*lundi*' underneath.

Getting up, he clicked out of the software, nodded to the policeman sitting opposite and made his way to Pelletier's office. Bruno wasn't there. Jacques ripped a page from his notebook, scribbled the details of his latest find along with a note about where he was going next, and left it on the magistrate's desk.

Back out on the street he crossed the ring road and within ten minutes was back in the general office at Vaux Investigations.

"We have something urgent to check," he said as he crossed the room to Didier Duclos' desk. "The Pierre Mancelle abduction—"

"And it is certain it is an abduction now, is it?" Didier sat back in his chair. A former policeman who had retired early from the force to care for his terminally-ill wife was now general office manager, investigator, and Jacques' deputy in his absence.

"I am, Didier," said Jacques as he pulled out a chair and sat down. "I've seen the CCTV footage from the school for yesterday. But I've also checked some of the previous footage. On Monday there was someone on a scooter outside the school grounds. Only part of the front wheel is in shot and then possibly the back wheel as the bike is turned around. I've left a note for Pelletier and suggested to him that a detailed list of owners in this area might be useful. I'll need you to follow up on that, please. I'm going to the school to talk to Madame Piquet and then on to Messandrierre to check on Marie. I'll be back last thing this afternoon." As he reached the office door, he turned. "You're old snouts, Didier. I want every single one of them working for us on this."

"Already done, Jacques."

wednesday, september 19th, 13.37

Jacques was ushered into the staff room by the school secretary and asked to wait. He dumped his helmet and bag on the only chair that was not already covered in coats, bags, exercise books or newspapers. As he glanced around the room he decided that the messiness must be an engrained feature. He moved across to the windows to wait. As he surveyed the playground beneath, the pavement and road beyond that was bounded by trees and shrubs, he realised how easy it would be for one of the children to be whisked out of sight in a moment. The trees and shrubs signified the edge of the wood that covered the area between Badaroux and Messandrierre. It was extensive and dense, and used for hunting. A chill ran along his spine as he thought of the other boys. The dead boys. His thoughts were interrupted by the secretary who ushered in Madame Piquet.

"Monsieur Forêt, how can I help?" The teacher, a small woman in her forties, advanced towards him, her hand outstretched in greeting. Her grip was firm when she took his hand. "Please sit," she said as she cleared a stack of exercise books from one chair and dumped them on the next. Sweeping a newspaper from another chair to the floor, she sat.

"Madame Piquet, I know the police have already spoken to you but I have some more detailed questions if you don't mind. Yesterday, when Pierre was taken, where were you?"

"I was in the entrance hall with the children still waiting to be collected. We don't like to let the children hang around in the playground if their parents or relatives are delayed."

"Can you tell me exactly what happened?"

"I had the twins with me. Their father always collects them on the first two days of the week and he is almost always late. Their grandmother picks them up the rest of the week." She smiled.

Jacques looked up from his notebook expecting her to say more, but her expression suggested to him that she thought she had delivered information of the greatest importance.

"Alright, you were with the twins. Were you talking to them? Or just waiting with them?"

"We were talking, as always. They are very bright little girls."

Jacques noticed her warm smile and wondered if the twins might be teacher's pets.

"So, I assume that means that you did not notice what Pierre and his sister might be doing in the playground?"

"That's right. I only became aware that Pierre was still waiting when he came back into the entrance hall with Célestine."

Jacques nodded. "And what did he say to you? If you can be as precise as possible that would be very helpful."

Madame Piquet smoothed her hand across her black skirt. "Pierre spoke first to his sister and told her to wait for their *maman*. When he spoke to me it was to ask me 'to look after Célestine for a minute'. Then he turned to go, but seemed to change his mind. Speaking to his sister, he said he 'would be back soon'. Next, he ran out of the door."

"Did you see where Pierre went or what he did?"

"I watched him as he ran down the steps at the entrance but my attention was diverted by Célestine who came to my side and took my hand. She's not a very confident little girl, Monsieur Forêt."

Jacques looked up from his note taking and nodded. "And what happened then?"

"I started a conversation with the twins and I actively encouraged Célestine to join in. The twins' father arrived and then Madame Mancelle came through the door immediately after him."

"Thank you, Madame. I'd like to move onto something else," said Jacques as he flipped back through his notes. "At lunchtime on the 17th, the day before Pierre was abducted, where were you?"

"I was here. I'd prepared my own lunch at home and brought it with me. It wasn't my turn for playground duty that day and I had some books to mark. I like to bring my own lunch whenever I can."

Jacques smiled. "So you ate first and then worked?"

"No, I ate and worked. I had seventeen books to mark."

"Did you remain in here throughout the lunch break?"

"Yes I did. I was working at the table over there by the window."

"And when the bell went for the end of playtime, what, exactly, did you do?"

"I hadn't quite finished my marking so I continued with that for maybe two or three minutes. It was the last exercise book."

"And then what? Take me through it step by step, please."

Madame Piquet got up and went over to the table. "I was sitting here." She pulled out the chair and sat down. Using her hands she mimed her actions as she spoke. "I closed the last book, and then I put it on the pile of already marked books. I collected them up and tidied them." Automatically, she stood, her arms cradling a pile of imaginary exercise books.

"Just hold that position, please. From there you would have been able to see out of the window and into the yard. What did you see?"

"Nothing in particular. The children. I heard one of my colleagues shouting to one of the boys. Oh! Of course. I've just remembered. Two scooters."

Jacques was on his feet and joined her at the table. "Where were they?"

"One was in the shadows of those trees, just over there." She pointed to the narrow track that snaked into the wood at the northern side of the playground. "The other scooter was closer to the school gates. About there," she said pointing half way along the railings to Jacques' right. "He was facing this way but he was on the far side of the street."

"You said 'he'; are you able to describe the driver of the scooter?"

Madame Piquet closed her eyes for a moment. "No, I'm afraid I can't." She let out a frustrated sigh. "They were wearing helmets, and jeans. One had a dark green waterproof jacket on. That's all I can remember."

"But you are certain that they were both male?"

"Certain? No, I'm not certain. I can't be certain, Monsieur, I didn't see their faces."

"But there must have been something that made you think they were male?"

"Their clothes, I think and the way they held themselves."

"So the scooter that was closest to the school fence. The one on the opposite side of the road just over there, he would be out of the range of the CCTV."

"Yes, I expect so. But he kept moving, a metre or so left and then back and then edging a little further forward and then away again."

"And the one in the shadow of the trees over by the track into the woods?"

Madame Piquet shook her head. "He was too far away for me to see in any detail. But the way he sat on the scooter suggested to me immediately that he was male."

"And the scooters? Can you describe them?"

"I don't know, one was a kind of dull grey and the other was blue, that's all I know."

"Any idea of the make or model?"

"I really couldn't say, Monsieur. They looked like those ones that have suddenly become popular again. Go to Mende in the evening at the weekend, you'll see them all over town."

"Alright, thank you. Then what did you do?"

"Umm... I had my books. Oh yes, I bent down to pick up my handbag and then I went to my locker."

"Did you look out of the window again?"

"No, but I'm sure the scooters were gone."

"How do you know that?"

"Perhaps I just heard them. I don't remember seeing them leave. But now I think about it, I'm sure they were gone."

Jacques made a final note and was about to tuck his pocketbook in his bag when Madame Piquet spoke.

"The man with the dog," she said, a look of horror on her face. "I completely forgot about him."

"What man?"

"There's a man with a white dog that has a large tan coloured patch on one side. He walks past the school every day just as the children are going home. Everyone knows him. The children call him *Monsieur Souris* because the patch on the dog is shaped like the head of Mickey Mouse."

"Did you see him yesterday?"

Madame Piquet frowned. "I'm not sure."

"What about his real name and an address?"

"I've no idea, Monsieur, and I've always assumed that he lives here in Badaroux because..." She shrugged. "I suppose he could live anywhere between here and Mende. I don't know."

"But he always walks his dog in the woods opposite at the same time every day?"

Madame Piquet nodded. "Yes. Every day, of that I am certain."

Jacques smiled and stood. "Thank you. You've been very helpful."

And I'll ask Didier to find Monsieur Souris.

"I'll see myself out." Jacques put his pocket book away. As soon as he was out of the room he pulled out his phone and called Didier. He listened to the ring tone as he ran down the stairs. By the time he was in the entrance hall, Didier had picked up the call.

"Didier, a new lead. Madame Piquet has just let me know that there is a man who regularly walks his dog by the school every afternoon just as the children are leaving...

Yes that's right, 16.30. It seems innocent enough but he may have seen something… No, we have no name other than the nickname given to him by the children, *Monsieur Souris*… Yes, please. If you could be at the school about 16.15, observe and note what happens and then follow… Thanks."

wednesday, september 19th, 14.29

In Verdon-le-Grand, Monsieur Archambault Hervé finished the last of his coffee and placed the cup back on the saucer. Standing with difficulty, he paused for a moment, his left hand on the back of the dining chair to steady himself. He grabbed his walking frame with his right hand. Another pause. Deciding that he had his weight evenly balanced, he made his way across the short distance from the small square dining table to his usual place at the window. He looked over at number 38. A car was parked outside. *Hmm, he's back.* The old man fumbled in the pocket of his jacket for his notebook. It wasn't there. Glancing around he remembered that his daughter-in-law, Sylvie, had taken it from him and placed it on the dresser on the opposite side of the room. He struggled to stand again, and as he manoeuvred the walking frame around he bumped into the small occasional table that sat permanently at the side of his armchair. It rocked and clumped onto the carpet. He cursed under his breath. Straining to hear, he recognised the sounds of washing up from the kitchen at the back of the house. *Good, she's still here.*

"Sylvie," he shouted as best his voice weakened by emphysema would allow. "Sylvie, I need your help, please." He slumped back in his chair.

A woman in her late fifties, with bright blue eyes and hair greying under the blonde dye, appeared in the doorway.

"*Papa*?" She glanced around the room as she tucked the tea towel into the pocket of her apron. Coming towards him, she righted the table and picked up the spilled contents: a pen, a detective story that he was half-way through, a pair of reading glasses, the day's newspaper and the TV remote.

"He's back. I told you he would be back." He picked up the spectacles. "Could you pass me the... umm the..." He struggled to find the word. "The paper thing... the..."

Sylvie went through her usual routine. "This?" She held up the newspaper.

Archambault shook his head. "No, the other paper, the over-there paper."

"This?" She passed him the notebook in response to his nod. "I suppose you will need this too," she said handing him the pen.

Archambault settled in his chair in front of the window and moved the edge of the net curtain to one side.

"He's back, you know. I told you he would be back."

"Who is, *papa*?"

"Old Vauquelin. He's back. I told you he would be."

Sylvie flopped down onto the empty dining chair. "Please, not this again," she muttered. She reached forward and tapped the old man gently on the knee.

"*Papa*, look at me." She waited for Archambault to face her. When he did she looked straight into his eyes. "Old Vauquelin is dead. He's been dead for almost twenty years and the rest of the family have moved away. No one has come back, *papa*. The house has been empty for years because the two sons won't agree to sell. Not that they'd get much for that place, the state it is in," she said more to herself than to her father-in-law.

The old man shook his head. "No," he said. Lifting the corner of the curtain, he pointed across the road. "It's him. That miserly old bastard, Vauquelin. He's back. I told you he would be back."

Sylvie stood, pulled the net across the width of the window and stared at the property across the road. "Alright, *papa*, have it your own way. But that is just a parked car. That's all. Just because the car is there it doesn't mean that someone is in that particular house." She straightened the flimsy hanging and smiled. "I'm going to finish the washing up and then I will have to go to collect your great-grandson from school. Will you be alright?"

Archambault nodded and continued to stare out of the window at number 38.

wednesday, september 19th, 15.01

Jacques parked his motorbike outside the Mancelle house in Messandrierre. Marie's car was parked in front of the garage. Carrying his helmet, he went to the door and knocked. Marie answered in a second, almost as though she had been standing on the other side waiting for him, or someone, to bring her some news. She ushered him into the lounge.

"How are you and Martin?" He watched as her face crumbled into tears. She fumbled in the sleeve of her oversized cardigan for a handkerchief.

"I just want to know where he is and that he will be coming back to us safe and sound, Jacques. That's all I want." She dabbed at her eyes and nose.

"And Martin?"

"He wants Pierre back, just as I do but he also wants justice. He left for the apartment in Marseille just after the press conference this morning and he's going to stay there. We thought it would make sense if there were always one of us at either place just in case Pierre turns up unexpectedly. I don't want him to arrive either here or at the apartment and find no-one home."

Jacques nodded. "I understand, but you both need to think about yourselves too. Have you eaten today?"

"A little. I'm all right, and I've cancelled all my private pupils and my classes for the foreseeable future, Jacques. I can't work not knowing where Pierre is." She sat next to Célestine and placed her arm around her daughter's shoulder.

"And I take it Célestine won't go to school without Pierre either."

"I tried to encourage her to go this morning but…" Marie shook her head, "she won't leave my side." Marie brushed away a stray tear.

Jacques nodded and glanced from the mother to the child. They both had red and swollen eyes with dark patches underneath. Marie's face was devoid of all make-up and her hair looked as though it had not been combed. Her expression was care-worn and worried.

"I'm sorry, but I have no news, yet. It's too early in the investigation. But, I do have some more questions for you." Jacques pulled out his notebook and pen.

Marie nodded.

"Have you undertaken a thorough search of Pierre's room to see if anything is missing?"

"The police asked me that too. And there's nothing. His room is exactly how he left it yesterday morning before he went to school."

"May I see it?"

Marie nodded. "Through there, you know the way."

Jacques moved through the house to the bedroom. Ignoring the threat on the label on the door he pushed it open and paused at the threshold for a moment as he cast his eyes systematically around the space. The bed, against the wall on the right, was partially made. The duvet was roughly thrown across it and the pillow was where it had been as Pierre had slept on it, the slight indentation created by his head still just visible. To the left of the bed was the window that overlooked the valley and below that a desk and a chair for Pierre to use for his schoolwork. The desk was untidy and covered in papers, books and a few toys from a previous period of his childhood. *Favourites.* Jacques grinned to himself as he thought about the room he had had as a boy in his parents' apartment in Paris.

Along the wall on the left were a chest of drawers, a small wardrobe, some bookshelves and a basket containing balls, games and other bits of playtime paraphernalia. Jacques pulled out his phone and took shots of the room.

Retrieving a pair of evidence gloves from his pocket, he

began a detailed search of the area and its contents. He wasn't entirely sure what it was he was looking for but he knew, from personal memory, where a nine-year old boy would be likely to stash things he didn't want his parents or little sister to find. Under one corner of the mattress were a couple of copies of a magazine about animals. Beneath the bed was a shoebox with all kinds of bits and pieces that Jacques considered to be of no consequence – some old toy soldiers, a rubber duck, a small metal car, some pencils and crayons, a pencil sharpener and bits cut out from magazines. He carefully replaced the box, a smile on his face as he wondered what his own mother had thought of the similar treasure chest that he had once kept under his bed.

The window sill provided seating for an old teddy bear, three robotic monsters from a movie for children that had been popular three or four years ago, and a couple of plastic dinosaurs. Jacques frowned as he picked them up. He had never understood the fascination with extinct species. His frown moved to a grin as he recalled one Christmas Eve with his nephews and the rest of the family in Paris. Thérèse's youngest boy had had a collection of dinosaurs too. Carefully replacing them, he was still unsure of what their attraction might be.

The desk took more time as he sorted through bits of paper, sweet wrappers, diagrams for who knew what and scribbled notes. On the front of a comic he noticed some doodles and examined them closely. As he turned the comic round he found some feint notes in pencil along the edge. Retrieving his notebook he copied the text and then recorded the actual text as a photo on his phone.

In the top drawer of the desk he found Pierre's toy fingerprinting kit, along with some rubber gloves.

"Just what every young detective needs," said Jacques addressing the teddy on the sill before he began rummaging around at the back. The drawer beneath was full of pens, pencils, crayons, paper and a very official looking policeman's notebook. Jacques smiled as he carefully replaced what had been his present to Pierre for his eighth birthday the year before.

Turning to his left, he scrutinised the shelves. A ceramic moneybox in the shape of a football was at one end of the top shelf. *Safely out of the reach of Célestine I suppose.* Jacques grinned to himself as he recalled the strategies he had once employed to hide his things from his sister. He rattled the moneybox, and the coins made a satisfying mellow sound. *Quite full, then.* He flipped through the pages of each of the books and only a folded sheet of paper containing a half-completed grid to work out a code floated to the floor. A second pile of magazines also revealed nothing of any importance. Satisfied that he had searched every centimetre of the room, he re-joined Marie in the *salon*.

"Did the police take Pierre's tablet?"

Marie thought for a moment. "I don't remember... I can't even recall them asking about it. His phone, yes, they asked a lot of questions."

"But the tablet?"

Marie shook her head and stared at the floor. "No," she said looking up at Jacques. "I'm certain they didn't ask about that."

"Is it still here?"

"Yes, I suppose so. I don't think he took it to school yesterday."

"It's not on the desk in his room."

"It isn't?" Marie's face looked vacant.

"There may be something on there that might be useful to the investigation team. Could one of his friends have it?"

"Oh, no, no. It'll be in his secret drawer. When he accepted that Célestine would be living with us on a permanent basis he asked for somewhere special to keep his tablet. He said his police work would need to be kept secret. So I had the *ébéniste* from Langogne come and have a look at his desk. There's a recessed space underneath the two main drawers. I'll show you."

In Pierre's bedroom Marie got down on her knees and applied pressure to a board at the bottom of the plinth under the drawers. As she moved her hand back, the front fell open.

"Yes, it's still here," she said as she reached in, pulled out the small tablet and handed it to Jacques.

"Thank you. Do you know if he has a password or user name?"

"No, Martin takes care of all of that. I know he has access to Martin's social media pages and he has a profile of his own, too. They message each other regularly when Martin is away. He misses his father a lot, especially now that he's growing up so fast."

Jacques frowned. "Pierre has a presence on social media? I thought he would be too young."

"He is, but all his friends at school have their own profiles. Martin set it up for him and he monitors the conversations."

"And have there been any incidents on social media that may have caused Pierre to leave or forced him to take any unusual decisions or actions?"

"I don't think so. Martin would have said if there had been. But, now you mention it, Pierre has been much quieter…more introverted, than usual, recently. I thought it was just his way of dealing with the massive change within the family over the last year. Before we adopted Célestine, Martin and I spent weeks, months discussing the impact of bringing her into the family and what it might mean for Pierre. We knew it would take all of us some time to adjust."

"And has Pierre adjusted well?"

"Yes, I think so. You've seen how protective he is of his little sister. The extra responsibility seems to be doing him good. But he's growing up, Jacques. He's asking very searching questions. Sometimes I know he knows the right answer and it feels as though he's testing me. At other times he asks questions that I think he feels he has a right to know about. In those situations I'm honest with him and I explain what he wants to know, but I also let him know whether he can repeat the information at school or not."

Marie looked down a second as a slight colour appeared on her cheeks. She smiled at Jacques.

"I was just thinking about my last...umm...awkward conversation with him. It was only three days ago. He's getting very curious."

"Just a couple more questions, Marie. I noticed some scribbles on bits of paper on Pierre's desk. Does the word or name 'Tomo' mean anything to you?

Marie stared out of the window as she thought for a moment. "No I don't think so. But there is a boy at school called Tomasz. Might it be a nickname for him?"

"Do you know his surname?"

"Not really, Pierre always refers to him as Tomasz Lech. I think his proper name is much longer than that."

Jacques made a note. "OK. I'll speak to his teacher, Madame Piquet, when I get back to Mende and check the correct name with her. His previous school, Marie, I remember you telling me there was someone there that Pierre had taken a strong dislike to. He didn't tell me much about it, but from what little he did say, I thought he may have been bullied."

"Yes, he was. That boy was in the year above Pierre and his name was Daniel St-Jean."

"He's not at Pierre's current school, is he?

"No, and if he was I would move Pierre again. That boy had a nasty, vicious streak to his character."

"Has Pierre mentioned him to you recently?"

Marie looked at him. "You don't... You're not saying he might be behind this, are you, Jacques?"

"No, but I think it is a line of enquiry that should be followed up. Do the investigation team know about Daniel?"

"No. I never thought to mention it. Pierre has been so much happier since he started at the school in Badaroux, until just recently."

"Just recently?"

"This last couple of months or so when he's been, more introverted. But, as I said, he's growing up, you know."

"Thanks, Marie, I'll see myself out." He forced a bright smile across his face. "We're doing everything we can."

It wasn't enough. He knew that. He also knew that there were no words of comfort to cover the unfathomable loss of a child. At the front door he stopped and asked himself if he had missed anything. *No.* He pulled the door open and gently closed it behind him.

Outside again, Jacques glanced at his watch. He had somewhere else to be but he also recognised that Madame Piquet would be leaving school soon. He pulled out his phone and rang Maxim.

"Maxim, something urgent has come up. Can you get in touch with Madame Piquet at the school in Badaroux and ask her if the word or name 'Tomo' means anything to her… Yes, it's T-O-M-O… Can you also ask about a boy called Tomasz Lech… Yes, and make sure you get his full name, please."

Business dealt with he didn't bother with his helmet. He released the steady on the bike and pushed it up the street, past the church and round onto the top road. Taking the top road out of the village had become his habit every time he was in Messandrierre since the end of the case centred in Montbel, a nearby village. He pushed on along the road until he came opposite *Ferme* Sithrez, still empty and, after three years, looking desolate and silent. He stopped and parked the bike. Leaving his helmet on the seat he walked the few metres to the top of the track leading down to *Ferme* Delacroix. Now that the old barn had been demolished and the house renovated, he could halt at the entrance to the track and see the property clearly. Jacques retrieved his notebook, turned to the back page and looked over an extensive list of notes. He glanced across the expanse of the property. The black convertible that Delacroix had bought the previous year was not in its usual spot. The blinds on the remodelled attic, which had become Delacroix's primary living space with full width windows, were closed. Jacques looked back over the last few entries.

Apparently not in residence since last week.

"So, where are you, Richard Laurent Delacroix?"

He returned to his bike, donned his helmet, straddled the machine and turned the key in the ignition. The bike roared along the top road to the sweeping junction with the D6 to Rieutort. As he paused to check the traffic, he made a mental note to talk to Maxim about Delacroix as soon as he got back to his office. The road was clear as he powered the bike down the D6 to join the N88 on his way to Mende. He had an important appointment that he could not miss.

wednesday, september 19th, 16.27

Didier had positioned himself on the track that led from the school in Badaroux into the forest. He was crouched down above the track and hidden in the undergrowth where he was waiting for *Monsieur Souris* and his dog.

At exactly 16.28 *Monsieur Souris* turned the corner and stopped. The dog sniffed at the corner of the wall surrounding the schoolyard. By the time the animal had had enough the children were beginning to spill out of school. *Monsieur Souris* continued a few steps further. He stopped to talk to a waiting parent. The triple kiss on the cheeks let Didier know everything he needed to know.

"Family," he muttered to himself. "His daughter, perhaps. Or daughter-in-law, maybe." He made a note of her description and continued watching.

A moment later and a child of about seven ran over with a couple of friends. The girls began fussing the dog, which lapped up the attention. *Monsieur Souris* chatted to the woman for a further ten minutes during which time the two girls who were not family had been replaced by four boys. Yet again the dog became the centre of attention and *Monsieur Souris* seemed to enjoy their company. A car drew up and one of the boys ran over and got in.

Monsieur Souris' possible daughter and the remaining girl and one of the boys then left. With his back now towards Didier, the man squatted down and continued chatting to the remaining two boys. Didier made notes and jotted down descriptions of the children. He wanted to be sure he could recognise them again. After a couple minutes, a young woman in an overall arrived. Didier felt sure he recognised the colour combination, but couldn't quite place the company name. He focused his binoculars on the decal on the front of her clothing.

"Just as I thought. She works at the tyre place just a few streets away." He made another note. With no more distractions, *Monsieur Souris* and his Jack Russell moved on across the road and along the pavement on the other side towards the track. Didier noticed he walked at a leisurely pace and, as he checked his watch, decided to give him a five-minute start before following. He packed his binoculars into his small rucksack and made his way down the slope, through the undergrowth and scrub and onto the track. He checked his watch. *Monsieur Souris* was about three minutes ahead.

Didier feigned interest in tightening his walking boot laces and then set off at a steady even walking pace. The track rose gently and followed a sweeping curve into the forest. After about four hundred metres, although Didier couldn't see his mark he could hear him whistling to his dog. He stepped up his pace. Another hundred metres and the track opened out into a small clearing. *Monsieur Souris* sat on the stump of what had once been a large chestnut tree, smoking and looking at something on his mobile phone. His dog was nowhere to be seen. Didier slowed his pace and continued.

"Monsieur, *bon après-midi*," said Didier as he drew level. *Monsieur Souris* snapped the cover of his phone shut and looked up.

"Monsieur." The greeting was almost inaudible and accompanied by the slightest of nods. He whistled for his dog and got up. "Fi!" he shouted. "Fi come here."

"If your dog is anything like mine used to be, she'll only come back when she's ready." Didier grinned. The man glanced at him and moved a couple of steps further away and continued to whistle and call for his dog.

"Need some help finding her?"

"No, thank you." He took a couple of steps up the bank. "I know where she'll be." He nodded again and strode in between the trees. Didier watched as the man marched away.

"Shit," he muttered under his breath as he moved out of the clearing and into the undergrowth. He'd have to sit this out.

It was another twenty minutes before *Monsieur Souris* returned to the clearing. His dog back on the lead, he took the path leading out of the wood and back towards the school. Didier followed a safe distance behind. The man emerged from the forest and retraced his steps past the school. When the dog stopped to sniff at the corner of the wall, Didier waited on the edge of the track. A moment later the man and his pet strode onto the main road through the town. Didier followed. An address was all he needed.

wednesday, september 19th, 17.42

The evening newspapers carried the story of Pierre's abduction. His photograph and the description of the clothes he was wearing were on every front page. As seventeen-year-old Olivier sauntered past the newsagent's on *boulevard* du Soubeyran in Mende he stopped. The childish face that was smiling out at him was familiar. Too familiar. He downed a large gulp of the fizzy liquid in the can he was holding and stared at the headlines.

"New Brat!" He pushed the can into the large square pocket of his grubby green coat and grabbed a copy of the paper. Screwing up his eyes and concentrating hard on the first few lines, he read slowly, the uncorrected astigmatism in his right eye distorting the words and letters. "That's stupid little New Brat!"

"The cost's a euro," came a gruff male voice from inside. "And this isn't a library." The owner moved to the doorway, a menacing look on his face. "Pay up or hop it!"

Olivier flung the paper at the man's chest and bolted across the road. A few metres away he slowed to a steady jog. The pain in his left side had come back again and he shoved his right arm inside the coat and around the bottom of his ribs. *A few more steps*. He turned into *place* au Blé in the old town. Sprawling on the wooden bench in the small square he tried to get his breath. He pulled the oversized coat around him. Not for warmth, the light September air still held the vestiges of the heat of the warm afternoon. He just needed to dull the pain in his ribs.

The splashed contents of the can had made a damp brown patch on the pocket that was sticky to his touch. Retrieving the can, he set it on the bench and used the sleeve of his coat to rub the latest of many grubby marks on the material. The dark tacky patch remained. Abandoning his task, he pulled his phone from his other pocket.

"Better see what's online," he muttered to himself. He scrolled through his news feed. "OMG! It's everywhere." Every site he accessed carried the same story and the same smiling photo of Pierre surmounted with headlines a variation on the one he'd seen in the newspaper – 'Opera Singer's Son Abducted'.

"OMG, what am I going to tell Tomek?" He wrapped both arms around himself and began to rock backwards and forwards. His eyes focussed on nothing, his breathing still a little ragged, the phone inert and resting on the bench beside the can.

"It was better before," he said. "When it was just me and Lavoie, it was better." A cold shudder shot up his spine as his associate, Tomek, crashed into his thoughts. Momentarily, he relived the most recent beating he'd been given. The beating that had caused the pain in his ribs. Grabbing the can for comfort he took another gulp. *What am I going to tell him?* As he drained the dregs of the drink a single common word from the web articles and the newspaper slowly began to break through into his jumbled, fretful thoughts and demand his attention. *Got to do something that makes me look smart.* A determined look on his face he concentrated on his phone and began typing a message to Tomek.

Olivier let a broad grin spread across his face as he pocketed the device. *I can fix this.* He dropped the empty can onto the paving stones beside the bench. As he toed it up the step onto the pavement behind the seat, it made a hollow clatter. A swagger in his gait, Olivier kicked the can ahead into *rue* de la République.

"I'll have this all worked out by the time I get to the squat." The can suffered another belt from his right foot and there was a muted clank as it careered along in front of him and came to rest against a large earthenware pot, adorned with autumn-flowering plants, halfway along the street. Still focussed on the can he continued into another small square and on towards the main street.

"'Bout time," sneered Tomek as Olivier appeared through the small access door in the metal shutter that had once secured the derelict warehouse. A copy of the evening newspaper landed at one side of the large empty crate that they used as a makeshift table. "We've got a problem and you're gonna fix it." Olive-skinned and dark-haired, Tomek fixed his dark brown eyes on Olivier. He was not a man to be challenged.

Olivier slumped down on the abandoned broken office chair. "Don't know what you mean."

"Look 'ere." Tomek was on his feet and moving around the crate. He opened out the folded journal with his left hand and placed it in front of Olivier. With his other hand he grabbed the back of Olivier's head and pushed his face to within a few centimetres of the newspaper. "Look!"

Olivier tried to lift his head but Tomek applied more pressure. "All right, get off me!" He tried to grab at the hand holding him but Tomek, the taller, stronger and older of the two, thumped his victim's face onto the hard wood of the frame of the crate. When he heard the scrunch of cartilage he let out a roar of laughter.

"What did you do that for?" Tears were pricking at Olivier's eyes when he raised his head. Using the back of his hand to staunch the flow of blood, he flinched at the touch.

Tomek was back in his scruffy and mouldering armchair, his black army-booted feet resting on the edge of the crate. "Cos I can and cos yer needed teaching a lesson." He smoothed a hank of greased hair back into its position.

Olivier swore under his breath.

"What? Yer got something to say?"

"No." The blood was still draining down his face and Olivier ripped a corner from the front page of the paper and held it to his nose.

"Good. New Brat, get him replaced and get rid of him. We can't 'ave him recognised. Set him to run. Saturday. But get it sorted, tonight."

Head held back Olivier took a deep breath. "His dad's in

the opera. He'll be loaded. We can sell New Brat back."

"That's kidnap and ransom. Do yer know what prison sentence that carries?"

"That's only if we get caught."

Tomek shook his head. "Man, you're stupid. He's seen us. He knows where the squat is. He knows who we are!"

"So, we take the money and run. We can take ALL the money. No cut for the Boss and no work."

"It's the Boss who wants 'im gone."

"I've got it all worked out. If we ask for—"

"I said we're getting rid of 'im." Tomek stood and leaned forward over the crate. "Do yer want another pasting?" He flexed his right hand, the metal skull of the heavy silver ring on his middle finger glinting in the half-light.

Olivier shook his head. He'd still got the faded yellowing remains of some of the bruises from the last time Tomek had taught him a lesson. And the pain in his ribs. The pain was still there. "Alright," he muttered.

Tomek straightened to his full height and grinned. "That's more like it. Now, I've got a delivery to collect, so whilst I'm out, feed the brats and get on the phone and message everyone about Saturday. Usual meeting time and place." Tomek pulled three notes out of his wallet and placed them on the crate. "That's so you can feed the brats and this," he said holding up a fourth and pristine €100 note. "That's yours when New Brat's gone."

Olivier's eyes widened. He wanted to snatch the cash from Tomek. Bitter experience had proved that such a response would only give his partner yet another opportunity to taunt him or beat him. He kept his eyes on the money and remained still.

"Not interested, huh?" The note disappeared back into Tomek's wallet.

"No!" Olivier held his breath and stared at Tomek. The silence seemed to be never-ending. A sly smile slowly crossed Tomek's face.

"I'll 'ang on to it anyway. Just in case there's a…hitch, shall we say? Eh?"

Olivier's eyes narrowed. *Bastard!* He nodded.

"And we've got business in Le Puy tonight. Make sure you and the brats are ready."

"Yeah, I know." Olivier watched as Tomek strode out of the warehouse. He heard the clank of the metal door and only then did he move. His right hand grabbed the money and shoved it in his pocket. With his foot he lashed out at the crate and it skittered a short distance across the floor. "Bastard! It's me and the brats who take all the risks. NOT YOU," he shouted as he picked the newspaper from off the floor and hurled it at the door. "You just take all the cash. It's not fair!"

His energy spent, Olivier slumped into Tomek's armchair. *I need to get out of this place.* He pulled the handful of notes out of his pocket and stared at them.

"And I need money."

wednesday, september 19th, 18.32

In the Vaux building in Mende, Jacques and his team were in his office undertaking a round-up of the findings from all the investigations worked on during the course of the day.

"...the Eluard case should be resolved finally by the end of this week. There's no doubt in my mind that the husband is being unfaithful to his wife. We have plenty of photos of him meeting his lady friend—"

"So, why can't the case be discharged immediately?" Jacques interrupted.

"I'm still waiting for confirmation of the identity of the woman concerned."

Jacques raised an eyebrow. "I see. But you're sure you can resolve this soon?"

Didier nodded.

"Alright, next we need to discuss the developments in the Mancelle abduction. Maxim."

"Since the press conference this morning, we already have sightings in St Étienne, Lyon, Mende and as far north as Clermont. All are in the process of being followed up or have been dismissed. So far, the only sighting that we thought might have been genuine was the one in Lyon. A lady who recognised Monsieur Mancelle from a production a couple of years ago feels sure that she saw him and his son in a restaurant earlier today with another man. Her description of the second man is very sketchy."

"And Pierre's father, what does he say?"

"That she's wrong. Pierre hasn't been in Lyon since July when he and the whole family were there visiting friends and relatives. When I relayed the description of the second man to Monsieur Mancelle he said that he has no idea who the other man could be. He also stated that he has not seen or heard from his son today and that since arriving at their apartment in Marseille at around 15.30 he has not been out. He and Madame Mancelle want to make sure that at least one of them is at either of their addresses if Pierre—"

"Yes, it's alright, Maxim, Marie explained their strategy when I saw her earlier this afternoon. If Monsieur Mancelle got to the apartment at around 15.30, then he will have been on the *autoroute* between here and Marseille around lunchtime today. Did you check his precise whereabouts for the time of the sighting?"

"I didn't need to, Jacques. Monsieur Mancelle told me as he was talking that he left Mende about 11 in a hire car."

"So, although he was alone in the car we can rule him out as being the individual in the restaurant in Lyon. But I think that sighting is a dead end and a waste of our, and police, time as happens so often with these sorts of cases."

"There are still more sightings that are coming in which I need to work through. The publicity arising from the press conference has been good – everyone knows about Pierre, but it is also bringing us more work than we can handle."

"OK. Didier, if we need more admin help then bring in some of our other people."

Didier nodded and jotted a note.

"And Madame Piquet, were you able to speak to her?"

Maxim nodded and flipped through the various pages of scribbled notes on his desk. "Yes, this one," he said seemingly picking a piece of paper at random. He turned it on its side.

"Madame Piquet called me back after the children had left for the day. I asked her if the word or name Tomo meant anything to her. Her immediate response was 'No.' When I suggested to her that it might be a nickname for one of the children, she agreed that it could be but went on to say that she could not recall hearing it used either in class or in the playground. When I asked about Tomasz Lech she said that he was in the same class as Pierre and that they are friends. When I asked if it was possible that Tomo might refer to Tomasz, she said not. She then added that the children always refer to Tomasz by his full name."

"And what about his full surname, Maxim? Marie seemed to think that Lech was a shortened form of his surname."

"Lech is his surname, Jacques. Just Lech."

"OK. Didier, any news on the scooter owners?"

"The investigation team have a complete list of owners which they are working through to narrow down the names. I'm waiting for a tip off from my old colleague."

"And your old snouts?"

Didier shook his head. "Nothing yet. They will get in touch as soon as they have anything, Jacques."

Jacques ran his hands through his hair and sighed. "I know. It's just that every moment is critical and as time marches on the probability of finding him alive lessens."

A heavy silence filled the room. Maxim turned his head away from the discussion and in the direction of the large windows. Didier concentrated on his notebook whilst Jacques' mind focussed on the distress the family were suffering. He didn't need to check his watch to know that Pierre had been missing for more than twenty-four hours. But he did it anyway in the blind hope that he may have miscalculated.

"Alright," said Jacques. "Didier, the man with the dog. *Monsieur Souris*. What did you get, if anything at all?"

"I positioned myself just inside the edge of the wood and waited for him there. He turned up at 16.28. First he spoke to one of the parents and considering how they greeted each other I would say it was either his daughter or daughter-in-law. Whilst they were chatting, some kids came across to pet the dog. I thought that *Monsieur Souris* took a lot of interest in the children and—"

Jacques sat up straight. "Interest? In what way?"

"It was when he squatted down on one knee. He had his back to me at that point and he had his hand on the back of the boy stood closest to him. He kept turning to the child and talking to him. I didn't like the way he kept running his hand up and down the child's back."

"Could the child have been a relative?"

Didier thought for a moment. "I suppose that could be possible, but the woman he greeted like a member of the family had left by then, taking one of the boys, her son, I would guess, with her." Didier frowned and pursed his lips together. "But there was something else, Jacques. When he eventually walked into the wood he took the track to a clearing where there's a tree stump. I deliberately let him get ahead of me before I set off down the track to follow. When I got to the clearing I saw that he has looking at his phone. He hadn't heard me coming and when I spoke to him he instantly closed the cover on his phone. He was also very stand-offish."

"So you think he might not have wanted you to see what he was looking at."

Didier shook his head. "I don't know, Jacques. He wouldn't engage in conversation. He looked shifty, and my old policeman's instinct was piqued."

"*Monsieur Souris* may not be as innocent as we first thought. Do we have a name?"

"Not yet, but I do have an address. As I couldn't engage him in conversation I waited until he left the wood and followed him home. He lives near the church in an old, three-storey, stone property that is not in a good state of repair. I'll check the register of voters tomorrow."

Jacques nodded his approval. "Maxim, an important task for you." He pulled the tablet from his bag. "This belongs to Pierre and it needs to go to the police. But before we do that is there any way that you can copy what's on the hard drive without leaving a trace so that we can examine who Pierre has been in contact with over the last couple of months?"

Maxim took the device and switched it on. "There's always a trace, Jacques, whatever action we take," he said as he waited for the first screen to appear. "It's password protected. Do we know the access code?"

"I don't, but his father will. Can you contact him, please?"

Maxim nodded.

"We also have another line of enquiry. When Pierre attended his previous school in Châteauneuf he was bullied by an older boy called Daniel St-Jean. Can we make some enquiries please and get contact details for his parents. I will need to speak to them as early as possible tomorrow."

"I'll deal with that," said Didier as he made a note of the name. "Did you find anything useful from the search of Pierre's room?"

"Not really." Jacques flipped back through his pocketbook. "The note referring to Tomo was all that I thought might be useful. Having spoken to Marie and now that we have the view of Pierre's teacher I don't think it refers to any of his school friends. But I don't want to rule it out completely, yet."

"I've added it to the whiteboard already," said Maxim.

"And I'll keep it in mind as well as I'm working through leads," said Didier. "Anything else, Jacques?"

"For Pierre? No, I don't think so." Pulling the substantial file that had been on his desk since he arrived back in the office on Monday, he sighed. "There's just the Delacroix case." He opened his notebook at the back where his own list of notes about Delacroix was located and he ripped out the pages. Flicking through the file he found the printout of all the sightings of Delacroix in response to the numerous requests that the team had outstanding on various websites and social media pages.

"I realise that the Delacroix case is only watching and noting at this stage. But there are some steps that we can take to make the information we hold more streamlined and relevant. So, since last year, when we realised that Monsieur Delacroix was a person to watch, I have been noting down whether he was in the village of Messandrierre or not on each occasion I have been there. Maxim, you need to compare my notes with the list on the printout." Jacques glanced at his notes again. "This is a perfect example" he said underlining an entry with his pen. "On this day last year we know that Delacroix was in Messandrierre that afternoon because Beth had agreed to visit him at home to complete a photographic commission. She returned later the same afternoon and he was still there. That means the reports of the sightings that we've got for Nîmes and St Étienne for that same day are both false. Using my notes as a basis you now need to work through all of the alleged sightings and narrow the list down to those that are likely and possible. When you've done that we'll take another look."

Collecting together the pages from his notebook, he placed them on the top of the file contents, closed the cover and handed it to Maxim.

"Didier, a word please."

Maxim collected his papers together and left.

"You look tired, Jacques." Didier pulled his chair up to the other side of Jacques' desk.

Jacques grinned. "Yes, I feel it. *Petit* Lucien is making his presence felt!"

"Another couple of months and things will improve. How's Beth?"

"Exhausted, too, and my sister is still with us. But I'm worried, Didier. Beth isn't coping very well at the moment, which is why I took her to see the doctor earlier."

"The baby blues?"

Jacques winced. "That's what I thought at first, but some of her behaviour has been very erratic. My sister suffered from post-natal depression following her first child and she's recognised some of her symptoms in Beth's behaviour."

"That's much more serious, isn't it?" Didier frowned.

"It can be very serious. Although the doctor didn't seem too concerned about that possibility, he wanted to keep an open mind. He wants us to try some new strategies and to come back and see him in a month. My sister has also made a few suggestions that helped her to get through her depression. But, Thérèse has her own family in Paris and she really needs to be with them. I was wondering, if I took some more time off after the Mancelle case is resolved, would you be able to manage the whole team for a month or maybe longer?"

Didier took a long breath, his lived-in face giving nothing away. "Managing the team and the work I can handle, Jacques, but all the negotiating at board level that you've been doing…" He shook his head. "I won't lie. I've never wanted to work at that level or with people who operate in that kind of environment with its back-stabbing, internal politics and…" He threw his hands up in the air. "It's not me, Jacques, and at the age of sixty-two, I think I've earned the right not to need to change my attitude."

"The discussions about the buy-out are almost complete, Didier. Alain and I still need to talk at the end of this week to thrash out some minor details. But that's all. I don't expect that there will be a need for you to wade into that discussion."

Didier moved across to the windows and looked out. "Alright," he said after a moment. Turning to face Jacques, he added, "I can certainly manage the work of the team for a month or a little longer. But, much more than that, and we will need to bring in someone to handle the cases I would normally have taken on."

"Do you have anyone in mind?"

"Let me think about that."

Jacques smiled. He knew exactly where Didier's thinking would end. *Gendarme* Thibault Clergue, having completed more than the minimum number of years of service, was due to retire at the end of the month. Jacques acknowledged that Clergue was a good foot soldier given the right instruction, but he knew he would never make an investigator. His career in the rural *gendarmerie* with no promotion and a reluctance to work in other fields was a testament to that. *He'll be easily managed, though, if we do need him.*

Keeping his thoughts to himself, he said, "I'll leave you to make some tentative approaches." He glanced at his watch. "And I think it's time we both went home. Ask Maxim to call me immediately if he finds anything on Pierre's tablet."

wednesday, september 19th, 19.27

In Tomek's absence, Olivier had been thinking. The money he'd been given had been spent on a *croque monsieur* for each of the brats, a whole take-away pizza for himself and some beers, which he didn't share either. The other things he needed he just lifted when no one was looking. The remaining cash, he pocketed, though he wasn't absolutely certain that he would get away with keeping the extra money but...*if I don't mention it, maybe Tomek won't ask.* He tried to assure himself. But his next thought contradicted that.

"If he asks, I suppose I can just give him the spare €5 note," he said before taking another swig of beer from the bottle on the repositioned crate. *That'll leave me €13 and some change.* He shook his head.

"It's not enough." He drained the beer and letting his hand fall to just above the floor beside his chair, he relaxed his fingers until the bottle eased itself out of his grip and onto the smooth concrete. It rolled slowly away until it came to rest, with a dull clink, against Tomek's metal gun chest. Olivier gave the bottle a passing glance and reached for the last full one. Using his penknife he prised off the top and chucked it over his shoulder. He was about to take a long swallow of the cool beer when the nucleus of an idea planted itself. As he worked his way down the bottle, the nucleus divided, multiplied and grew into a misshapen, slightly opaque but believable fiction that he felt he could get past Tomek. He turned and stared at the chest. *Tomek keeps everything in there.* Another swig of beer and the idea taking shape in his conscious mind became clearer. *The phones, the sims and the guns.* A smile broadened across his face. *Tomek keeps everything in that chest.*

Abandoning the beer, he pulled out his phone, checked the time and placed his phone on the chest next to the bottle. *I can do it. I know I can do it.* Before moving across to the metal chest, he tiptoed to the small door in the shutter and ducked outside.

"Alright," he said as he surveyed the space next to the rusty white Peugeot van that they used for business. "Tomek's on the moped, so I'll hear him when he gets back."

He quickly ducked back inside and went straight to the chest. Even though his associate was nowhere close he still carefully and quietly drew back the bolts at the front. As he lifted the lid the hinges let out a rusty groan. Olivier held his breath. He felt the blood drain from his face. Slowly turning his head, he looked over his shoulder at the door and listened. *Shut and no sound of Tomek. OK. Come on, let's do this.*

The chest had two tiers. The first a shallow lift out tray divided into three sections. The section on the left contained mobile phones, sims, covers and other devices. Small sealed packets of drugs were at the opposite end and a small supply of ammunition was kept in the central section. Olivier searched through the first section until he found the phone he wanted. The white one that belonged to New Brat. Holding the bag upside down he tipped out the contents; the phone, the back, the cover and the precious small square of gold coloured metal that was the sim, fell onto the concrete floor. He retrieved the sim and placed it inside the handset. He fixed the back and front cover onto the phone and secreted it in the inside pocket of his coat. Next, he pulled out another bag. This contained a pre-paid phone that Tomek had purchased with cash. Holding onto the edge of the chest he took some deep breaths. *Need to leave everything just as it was.* He glanced over the tray in the chest and began rearranging the remaining phones and other devices. It looked exactly the same as before. About to close the lid he noticed the empty bag lying on top of the section with the ammunition. He snatched it out, shoved it in his pocket and slammed the lid shut.

Returning to the crate he collapsed into Tomek's armchair. With his hands jammed under his armpits he hugged himself until his heart rate began to slow to its more usual speed.

"I can do this," he said as he retrieved his own phone. As a reward to himself for his bravery, he logged onto his favourite gaming site.

"Now, let's see what we can do and then it's time to work."

It was almost 20.15 when Tomek returned. The heavy army boots had been exchanged for expensive looking brown brogues, the fatigues for designer jeans and the black shirt for a pale blue one and a navy jacket.

"All set?" Tomek strode across to the metal chest. "Give us an 'and with this," he said, bending down to take one of the handles. Olivier jumped to his feet and between them they carried the chest outside and placed it in the back of the white van. Tomek turned, "Right, let's get the brats."

Olivier followed a few steps behind as Tomek marched to the entrance to the small room at the end of the warehouse. He drew the bolts noisily and pulled open the door.

"Come on, get up, yer idle brats." Tomek kicked at each of them in turn as he carved his way through the three inert youngsters. Olivier remained at the threshold and watched. As expected Fierce Brat hit back and Tomek responded with a hefty belt across the face with the back of his right hand. Stupid Brat snivelled and tried to avoid Tomek's foot whilst New Brat scrunched himself up in the corner against the back wall of the tiny room. Even though he was trying to get up, he still got a hefty kick in the left thigh.

"Ah, it's New Brat. New Brat with 'is face all over the newspapers," said Tomek as he grabbed the front of Pierre's hoodie, pulled him forward and then slammed him into the wall behind. Pierre let out a winded yelp. He had a welt across his forehead. *Tomek again.* Olivier flinched as he recalled seeing New Brat slump to the floor, unconscious, as a result of the crack from Tomek's fist. *Seems all right now, though.* With Pierre pinned against the wall, Olivier noticed that there was a dark, swollen, patch around his left eye that was forcing his eyelid closed. Probably Fierce Brat, he thought.

"Trainers," demanded Tomek as he pulled a small gun from the back of his trouser belt under the jacket. "Off and give 'em 'ere," he said left hand held out, right hand holding his gun a few centimetres from the boy's face. Pierre squatted down to unlace them and Tomek shoved the flat of his left foot at his victim and pushed him over. "Kick 'em off, yer stupid…"

Pierre whimpered and without waiting Tomek grabbed a shoe and pulled at it and tossed it across the room. Olivier took a step forward and caught it. He watched as Tomek grabbed Pierre's other foot and yanked the second shoe off and tossed that across, too.

Both shoes in his hands, Olivier watched Pierre pull at his grey socks as Tomek towered over the boy. "You've been fed, so now you've got to work." Grabbing at Pierre's arm he pulled him up and put his gun to the boys back. "Move."

Olivier stood aside to let Tomek pass. "Leave Fierce Brat and bring the other one," Tomek said as he frog-marched Pierre across the warehouse and out into the waiting van. Olivier dropped the trainers and grabbed Stupid Brat. He gave no resistance, but Fierce Brat jumped up and tried to barge through the doorway. Olivier shoved him back, slammed the door shut and shot one of the bolts. He delivered the boy to Tomek who pushed him into the back of the van. Returning to get the trainers he heard Fierce Brat kicking at the door.

"Shut up. We know where your *maman* lives, so shut up." Olivier put his ear to the door and listened. Squatting down he closed the bolt at the bottom of the door and then looked through the tiny hole in a knot in the wood. Fierce

Brat was over by the back wall, his head in his hands, crying. Olivier grinned. Grabbing the trainers he ran out to the van.

***

Pierre was shoved and pushed out into a dark yard and then into the back of a battered and rusty van. He made for the side and sat on an old sack close behind the driver's seat. A long metal chest stood across the centre of the floor of the vehicle on his left. The night air was chilly and he wrapped his hands and arms around him for warmth. Tomek stood between the doors at the back watching him. He heard the clang of metal as the place where he'd been kept was secured. Tomek turned as Olivier appeared and shoved the second boy into the van. The double doors at the back were slammed shut and locked.

Pierre pressed his ears against the side of the van. He could hear footsteps but no one was speaking. The driver and passenger doors were opened and closed. The engine started. They were moving, but he didn't know where.

He glanced around. There were no windows in the back doors and when he turned to look out of the front windscreen, he saw a wall of tarpaulin. Pierre moved a little to his right. The tarpaulin didn't quite reach the floor of the van. He pulled at the corner and it came free. Behind was a metal square-meshed grill that divided off the front cab. He let the corner of material drop and rubbed the tears welling in his eyes away.

The other boy just sat there, silent, inert and huddled against the wall of the vehicle. His face and hair were dirty, his clothes grubby and creased. He was staring at the filthy floorpan. *I don't even know his name.* Pierre decided the boy looked lonely and inwardly debated whether the boy would respond if he spoke to him.

I must, I need to be able to tell Jacques when he finds me. He will find me.

That final thought kept running through his mind as the

vehicle swayed and moved. *I don't know where we're going.* The van took a sweeping bend to the right and both the occupants of the back and the chest slewed across the floor. Pierre sat upright first.

"Where are we going?"

Stupid Brat didn't respond. He didn't even acknowledge the question. Pierre asked in a slightly louder whisper. This time the boy looked up, shrugged and turned away.

Pierre moved back to his space between the metal chest and the wall of the van. Leaning his head against the side, he let the tears he had been holding back silently trickle down his face. *Monsieur Jacques will find me. He will know what to do.* Wiping his face with the back of his hand he let his mind run over everything that had happened since school. He closed his eyes. He wanted to make sure that he could remember everything. It was important.

thursday, september 20th, 01.18

Pierre's red and grey trainers, the laces tied together, were slung around the recently painted fencing above the river Le Dolaizon, a small tributary of the Loire on the south side of the old city centre of Le Puy-en-Velay. Pierre and the other boy were huddled under an arch of the bridge. Olivier was facing them but leaning against the wall support for Avenue Clemenceau above. He had his phone to his ear constantly talking to Tomek, or so Pierre thought, having overheard one half of the conversation.

Pierre knew exactly where he was. The avenue was the route his parents always used to come into the city. They came often. Sometimes to see friends, sometimes for his mother to shop and once, the previous year, to hear his father sing in the cathedral. The last visit with his mother was only the month before.

Tomek was above in the small open space mingling with the late night revellers who were issuing from the nightclubs across the city and making their way home on foot. The noise of traffic was light and Pierre could hear various voices.

Olivier, with his phone to his ear, was issuing orders and handing out small packets to the other boy. But his eyes never left Pierre.

I can run. If I can run, I can get home.

"You. New Brat."

Pierre jumped up as he realised it was his turn.

"Take this. Woman, green dress, black jacket, up by the tree. Be quick." Olivier pulled his gun from his grubby coat pocket. "I'm watching you," he said as the gun jabbed into

Pierre's back and Olivier followed him out from the cover of the arch and towards the steps to the road.

Olivier pushed the gun against Pierre's spine and placed the package in boy's hand. Remaining behind the back of the van, Olivier stopped.

"Up the steps," he said, "And no screwing up. Tomek's up there."

Pierre nodded and ran the short distance across the tarmac to the steps. His socks soaked up the moisture in a small puddle that had formed from some light rain a little earlier. He ran up the steps and spotted Tomek at the top. Looking around, he saw the tree at the corner of the widened pavement and vehicles parked in a side street beyond. The woman was leaning against the fencing surrounding a small planted area beneath the tree, smoking. Tomek, close to her right, was between himself and the woman, talking through his phone but watching. Watching intently.

Pierre sprinted the short distance, dropped the package into the woman's hand and ran back. The fleeting idea that he could keep on running until he got back home deserted him the second he saw Tomek pull his gun halfway out of his jacket pocket.

Back with the other boy, he sank down on the ground and rubbed his feet. They were sore and cold. When he pulled off one of his socks he saw little traces of blood where something sharp on the tarmac had pierced the soft skin of his soles. In the pale light from the moon and the low light from a streetlamp above, he pulled his sock back on and hunkered down inside his hoodie, hands in his pockets. Tomek and Olivier continued their business. Pierre waited his turn, tears in his eyes but willing himself not to cry openly. He tried to melt back into the wall of the arch as he watched Olivier and the other boy.

***

Olivier switched his phone off and slipped it into the outside pocket of his coat. He patted the top left section of the garment, making sure the two other phones were still there.

"'Ere," said Tomek as he tossed the van keys down to Olivier. He removed the trainers from the fence and let them drop down to land on the tarmac just beside where Pierre sat, out of sight of anyone on the road above. "I'm stayin' 'ere tonight," he said and winked. "Get the brats back and wait for me to come in tomorrow."

Olivier, confused at the sudden change of plan, stared at Tomek. "You're not coming?"

"Move yer dumb'ead." Tomek took the arm of the woman in the green dress who stood beside him.

Olivier took a step further out from the arch and caught a fleeting glimpse of Tomek and the woman walking away together.

"Right, got it." He smiled to himself as he picked up the trainers and slung them round his neck. "Get up, both of you, and get in the van."

He grabbed each of them by the upper arm and pinned them against the wall. "I'm in charge. Got it?" The boys nodded and Stupid Brat began to whimper.

"Stop snivelling." Olivier marched them both to the back of the van. "New Brat, open the door."

Pierre responded immediately and Olivier shoved him inside, swiftly pushing Stupid Brat in behind. The van doors were shut and locked. Getting into the driver's seat, he pulled a clip above his left shoulder and let the top corner of the tarpaulin drop down behind his seat.

"Not a word," he said, looking over his shoulder through the grill. He put the keys in the ignition and started the engine.

The route from Le Puy to Mende was empty. The odd taxi passed Olivier on the outskirts of the city, but that was as much traffic as he encountered. It was all that he wanted to encounter. With no *permis*, no formal driving lessons, and false plates, he knew he was the dream book for the local *flic*. Whilst in the environs of the city he kept rigidly to the speed limits. Once out on the *route nationale* he relaxed a little. The danger of being caught and booked wasn't gone, but it was much less likely. But Tomek was gone too. That was an unexpected bonus.

He glanced in his wing mirror. There was nothing but darkness. Turning his head a little to his right, he listened. *Brats asleep, I think.* Tugging at his seatbelt to slacken it, he repositioned himself and settled back in his seat. *Great, I can get away with this.* He grinned to himself.

"And I didn't even need my story to get rid of Tomek. He just got rid of himself." A belly laugh began to rise up from his stomach, but he forced it back down and allowed only a light snigger to emerge. "I'm rollin'," he murmured to himself. "I'm absolutely rollin'."

The road swerved and Olivier had to stab on the brakes. "Concentrate!" The van slowed a little as Olivier focused on the dark road ahead. He slid through the centre of Langogne – another sleepy mountain town that paid no attention to the early-morning visitor. The N88 extended up out of the town and wound its way through open countryside. Approaching Châteauneuf-du-Randon, Olivier began to feel unsettled. The moment he'd been waiting for would soon be upon him. He took a deep breath to help quell the nerves in the pit of his stomach.

The road wound round the foot of the rocky outcrop that supported the tiny fortified village of Châteauneuf. With other dark heights rising on his left he cruised along. Soon his route began to rise again towards the Col de la Pierre Plantée. *Not far now.* He flexed his shoulders.

"Can't stuff up now," he told himself. He checked the rearview mirror, just to re-assure himself that the two boys were still asleep. A glance in his wing-mirror and he confirmed that there was no-one following behind. Reaching the high point of the col, the road swept right and then left and began the short and slight descent towards the village of Messandrierre.

Olivier slowed, looking for the cross that marked the

entrance to the village. Hunched over the steering wheel he peered out of the window and slid the van into third.

"There. Yeah, that's it." He pulled off to the right, changed to second and pulled around the monument. The van stopped at the other side of the cross facing out to the N88. Olivier killed the engine.

Opening the driver's door as quietly as he could, he slipped out into the darkness. He pushed the door closed and locked it. He could feel his heart knocking against his chest at a couple of speeds faster than normal as he started to walk away from the van and along the short street. He wasn't sure of the address but he knew he would recognise the house when he saw it. He tip-toed along Grand Rue and up towards the church, looking to his left. He'd remembered that the house was on the left. He was sure of that. *It's that one.* He stopped and looked around. In the dark of the early morning the village was silent and empty. A cloud lazily shifted from in front of a pale moon. Olivier took a couple of steps further towards the house with the beautifully planted, but small front garden. *That's definitely it.*

Reaching into the pocket of his coat, he took out a crumpled square of paper and shoved it into the letterbox sited on the low wall that surrounded the property. He was careful to ease the flap shut rather than let it drop. Looking around again to check that he was alone, he soundlessly stole back through the houses; a slight, dark shadow in an oversized waxed coat that caught the sheen of hazy moonlight as he moved.

"Job done," he murmured as he slipped the key in the lock on the van.

thursday, september 20th, 06.14

Jacques had managed some sleep overnight but the overwhelming weariness that he felt was still there. The strong black coffee in his breakfast cup was helping, but only just. With the laptop on a corner of the table he was already working through his emails. Hearing the door to the room click shut, he looked up.

"Hello, little man," he said as he got up and moved across the room. "Does *maman* look a little better today, do you think?" Jacques took the baby and returned to his seat at the table.

Beth pulled out a chair and sat opposite them.

"I managed just over five hours' sleep," she said. "And yes, I am feeling a little better today."

Jacques smiled. He wasn't convinced. Beth still looked drawn and the dark marks under her eyes had not lessened in either extent or colour. He noticed that she was twisting her ring around her finger. He hadn't seen her do that for a long time. Although, now he considered it again, he realised that it had become a feature of the late stages of her pregnancy.

"Maybe you should let Thérèse take Lucien today so that you can rest a bit more and try out some of the advice the doctor offered yesterday." Lucien's tiny hand was searching the air and Jacques quickly responded by looping his little finger underneath it.

Beth's eyes were darting around the room. "Let me have him." She reached out across the table and then shook her head. "No, that's not what I…"

"I know. But he is safe with me, Beth, and he is safe with Thérèse. You can trust us."

She frowned. "I wanted to say something else, but I can't remember…"

"It'll come back to you." Jacques watched as Beth's frown dissipated. Her eyes fell on the child and she remained motionless. She began humming. The same three or bars over and over again. She seemed to be slipping further away from him.

"Pretty tune," he said. "I don't know it. Is it a family thing from when you were a child?" There was no response. "Beth?"

She turned to face him, her eyes vacant. "Yes?"

"Why don't you go and have a shower. I'll look after Lucien. And then, maybe today we can try taking him out. Perhaps you could meet me for lunch."

The confusion and distress on her face made him realise he had asked for too much too soon.

"Let me have him, Jacques." She was up and standing beside him, arms outstretched.

"He's safe with me, Beth, and I would like to spend a little more time with him before I go to work. Why don't you get showered? We'll still be here when you're finished."

She stroked her son's head. "You won't leave before I come back?"

"I promise."

She hesitated. "OK." Crossing the room, she turned in the doorway.

Jacques noticed that the vacant look was back.

thursday, september 20th, 09.15

A thin woman of average height opened the door to the apartment. Her clothes were cheap and well-worn, her hair dyed and the roots were in desperate need of attention.

"Madame St-Jean?"

The woman nodded, her expression unsure.

"I'm Jacques Forêt, previously of the Paris police and now working as a private investigator. May I come in?"

Madame St-Jean eyed him up and down but opened the door and gestured for him to enter anyway. The apartment was small. The living space included a galley kitchen and a combined lounge area. Jacques guessed the only other rooms would be a bedroom and a small bathroom.

"Please, take a seat," she said.

Jacques perched on the edge of a sofa that was barely adequate for two people. "I'm working for the parents of Pierre Mancelle who was abducted from outside his school two days ago. You may have read about it in the papers this week."

"Yes, I know about that."

"Your son, Daniel, Madame. I believe he and Pierre were friends at school."

Madame St-Jean reached across for her cigarettes from the coffee table that occupied more than its fair share of the available space.

"You could say that," she said putting a light to the cigarette.

"But what would you say, Madame?"

She took a long drag, held the fumes for a moment, and then lifting her head she filled the atmosphere with a blue haze.

"That if this is about that stuck-up mother of his trying to make out my son is to blame again, then no, they weren't friends at school." She sat back and crossed her legs. Her eyes were cold and defiant as she waited for the next question. The cigarette was left to smoulder between her nicotine-stained fingers.

Jacques took a different tack. "How is Daniel getting on at school, Madame?"

She returned her attention to the cigarette before answering. "I haven't seen him for six months. So, how would I know?"

"Do you know where Daniel might be now?"

She let out a snort of derision. "At school if he's got any sense, but I doubt it." A small amount of ash from the cigarette dropped onto the floor as she played with the stub.

"And where is Daniel living at the moment if he's not living here with you?"

"At his father's in St-Étienne." She took another lungful of smoke, held it and exhaled it into the room. Stubbing out the remains of her cigarette on a saucer on the chair arm she immediately reached for another one.

"And the address, please? It would be helpful if I could talk to Daniel."

"I don't see why. Daniel may be wilful and disobedient, but he hasn't the brain to mastermind a kidnapping. He takes after his father in the brains department." She got up and collected an address book from the kitchen counter.

"Here," she said pulling out a scrap of paper and handing it to him. "Take it, that's the last address I had. Six months ago."

"Thank you." Jacques pocketed the note and made his way out.

In the sunshine he stood at the bike and took deep breaths of fresh air, one after the other, pleased to be out of the claustrophobic, smoke filled atmosphere of Madame St-Jean's apartment. As he was about to get on his bike his phone rang and he picked up the call.

thursday, september 20th, 10.32

Sprinting up the stairs to the 4th floor of the Vaux Building in Mende, Jacques charged into the general office.

"A new line of enquiry, Didier," he said as he breezed into the room. Grabbing a spare chair en route, he dragged it with him to his colleague's desk.

"I've got some news, too," said Maxim looking up from his computer screen.

Positioning the chair at the side of Didier's desk, Jacques dumped his bag on it and strode back to where Maxim was working.

"What have you got?" Jacques peered over Maxim's shoulder and scrutinised the screen.

"I've been working through all the files on Pierre's tablet. The password is the name of the dog in the adventure stories on his bookshelf with the numerals 0806 added at the end."

Jacques grinned. "I should have been able to work that one out. Pierre loves those stories and he insisted on seeing the film they released last autumn."

"Yes, I know," said Maxim, a wide smile on his face. "Having seen your photos of his bedroom, I should have worked it out, too. But this is what I want to show you." He clicked on a colourful icon that represented a game. "I don't know if this is really relevant, but Pierre spends a fair bit of time playing this particular game. And he's quite practised at it, too." Maxim clicked through to the leader board. "This is Pierre, here. He's fourth at the moment," he said, using the mouse to highlight the name 'Hero0806'. "But it's this player's handle that I think we might need to look at." Maxim moved his cursor to the top of the leader board.

"Tomahawk571," Jacques read the name out loud. "Are you thinking that might be Tomo?"

"I don't know what I'm thinking, really, Jacques."

Didier joined them and peered over Jacques' shoulder at the screen. "Pierre's handle would suggest that the numerals are his birthday," said Didier.

"They are," said Jacques.

"So 571 could be the fifth month of 1971, or 57 being the year and 1 the first month," suggested Didier. "Which means we could be looking for a man who is 41 years old in the first instance or 55 years old in the second."

"But it can also mean that there are 570 other players using the name Tomahawk for this particular game," said Maxim. "When a new user chooses a name that someone already has the software that manages the game suggests an alternative and the easiest way to do that is to set up an incremental command like this." Maxim jotted down a line of a symbols and added '+1' on a scrap of paper.

Jacques glanced at Didier who shook his head. "Umm, I'll take your word for that, Maxim. But, I think what you're saying is that we might have a lead but that it could also go nowhere. Hmm... I would expect that anyone who is trapping youngsters through an online computer game would deliberately avoid a handle that could be interpreted as giving away any information about their real personal circumstances."

"But I can't stop thinking that Tomo and Tomahawk571 might be the same person. They also might be just another kid who has nothing to do with Pierre's disappearance." Maxim shrugged. "Should I follow it up? I've still got a lot of files and other stuff on here to go through."

"I think we need to find a connection that shows that Tomahawk571 is Tomo. Maybe there are messages between Pierre and either Tomahawk or Tomo. If there are then we need to examine the content of those messages to see if there is a connection. You need to keep Tomo or Tomahawk571 in mind, Maxim, as you work through everything else... And, when you both hear what I have to say, you may find you can make more informed decisions."

Jacques moved across the room to retrieve his bag. He flipped open the cover and pulled out an evidence bag which he set out on Didier's desk.

"This ransom demand was in the post box at the Mancelle house in Messandrierre. Marie found it this morning and telephoned me immediately. I called there on my way back here." He let them both read the note.

Didier picked up the bag and turned it over. "Was there no envelope?"

"No. According to Marie, Jean-Paul, the postman, still hadn't arrived in the village when she checked the post-box. And she only checked the post-box because she'd realised that she hadn't done so since the day before yesterday."

A gleam in his eye, Didier nodded. "Fingerprints," he said. "If only you and Marie have touched this, then we might be lucky."

"Yes, we might be," said Jacques. "If the sender didn't wear gloves, then we may have the prints of whoever has Pierre." Jacques let out a long, low sigh as he slumped into the chair beside the desk. "And if the investigation team have a match on file, then we may have a name. But we will still have to find Pierre's current location. And I would like to achieve that without Marie and Martin having to pay a single *centime*."

"There's something else," said Didier, a grave expression on his face. "If this didn't come by post, then it must have been delivered by hand and that—"

"Yes, I know," interrupted Jacques. "Whoever has Pierre, knows where he lives, and they could have got that information either by following him home from school before they took him or he could have given them the information himself."

"Either voluntarily or by force." Didier moved around to his side of the desk and sat. Elbows on the desk, he clasped his hands together and rested his chin against them.

Jacques looked at each of his colleagues. They both avoided eye contact. *You're exploring the same ugly question as me, aren't you?* He glanced at his watch. *Forty-three hours and counting.* He shook away the thought that it might already be too late for Pierre.

It was Jacques who broke the silence of the sombre stillness that had invaded the room.

"Alright. Let's try and stay positive. We have a boy to find and criminals to catch." Sitting up straight, he pulled the evidence bag across the desk and turned it over so that the back of the photograph that had been ripped out of the newspaper could be seen. "That photo was the one Marie gave to the investigation team. It's been copied to all the local papers in Lozère, to papers in the neighbouring *départements* and across the region of Languedoc-Roussillon. But what about these other stories, Maxim, can you identify the newspaper they came from?"

Leaning over the desk, Maxim ran his finger across bits of sentences and titles until he brought it to rest on one of the articles. "That looks like something from one of the evening papers from yesterday," he said. "We've still got them all. It should be easy to identify which one."

"Good. If we can identify the paper, we can identify a distribution area. It won't tell us where Pierre is but it is a start." Maxim nodded, crossed to the large filing cabinet and removed a bundle of newspapers from the third shelf. Dumping them on his desk he began his search.

"That wording on the scrap of paper attached to the news article, Jacques," said Didier, turning the bag to face them both. "It doesn't look right, does it?"

Jacques picked up the bag and closely examined the note. "You're right. It looks very amateurish."

Didier frowned. "The amount... I never worked any kidnappings when I was with the *police municipale*, but the amount demanded as ransom seems...unusual, to me."

Jacques nodded. "I agree. Why only ask for €13,400. Why not €20,000 or €50,000? Or more?"

"Could the note be a prank? Someone not connected with Pierre's disappearance but having seen the publicity, decided to take the opportunity to try and make some money?"

"It could be, and if it is, we need to know how they have Pierre's phone. The number quoted is definitely his."

"I thought kidnappers usually made videos of the victim," said Maxim as he joined the conversation at Didier's desk. "The day's newspaper somewhere in there as well. That's how it was done in a film I was watching a couple of weeks ago." He put a local newspaper on the desk.

"If you're dealing with a terrorist, Maxim, maybe. But there's nothing to suggest that here or with the other deaths that we've been tracking."

Maxim opened the first page of the newspaper and placed it next to the evidence bag, turning it so that the articles on the back of the photo could be seen.

"It's been ripped from the local evening news which is distributed across the whole of the *commune* of Mende."

Jacques compared the two pieces of newsprint, cross-checking the titles, a couple of printing errors and a corner of a small add. "It's a match," he said. "A perfect match and if we're lucky it might mean Pierre is somewhere close."

"You were talking about the amount," said Maxim as he flipped through towards the back of the paper. "I remembered something about money... Yes, in this article here." He folded the paper back and pointed to a small item that held a table of statistical and financial data.

Jacques looked from one to the other. "You're right again, thanks."

"We need to pass this on to the investigation team, Jacques, as quickly as possible."

Jacques frowned. "Yes, I know that, Didier, and we will pass it on, but not until I've spoken to these people on behalf of Marie and—"

"Hold on, Jacques!" Didier grabbed the ransom note. "If we delay we could find ourselves in breach of the law."

"Obstructing a police investigation? Yes, I've considered that and what I propose is that we get Maxim to take this across to the investigation team and whilst he is doing that I will contact the number given and then update the police in person immediately afterwards."

Jacques returned Didier's narrowed-eyed stare. *I need you behind me on this.* He waited. *Come on, Didier.* Jacques held his nerve.

"OK." Didier released his hold on the evidence bag. "We'll need a trace on the call and we'll need to record everything that's said."

"Let's get everything set up now," said Jacques. "I'll call the investigation team and let them know we are sending over some new evidence."

thursday, september 20th, 11.07

Olivier pocketed the phone. From the old cemetery in Mende it was a short walk down the hill to the river. From there he could make his way along the riverbank to the squat. He broke into a trot on the descending road to ensure he wasn't late. It was never good to be late for Tomek.

The road was quiet and the late morning sun was tempered by a slight, but fresh, breeze. Olivier had to pause at the bottom of the road. The pain in his ribs had returned. Hunched over, hands resting on his knees, he took a few moments to get his breath back. An elderly lady carrying some flowers crossed to the opposite pavement. Olivier just glared at her.

On again, he dodged the traffic on the main road at the bottom and disappeared into a short narrow street on the other side. Clambering onto a wall that stood waist-height, he dropped onto the riverbank behind it. Through the brush and undergrowth, beneath the bridge, and he would be back in the safety of the derelict warehouse in a few minutes. Climbing up the half dozen rotten wooden steps that had once led to a busy jetty, he stopped and looked around. *No one. Good.* He edged his way around the building and let himself in through the small metal door.

"Where've yer been?" Tomek was on his feet and across the floor before Olivier had time to stand up straight. Pinned to the metal of the large shutter with Tomek's hand around his throat, Olivier gagged. He squirmed to get free, hardly able to breathe. He worked his mouth trying to speak but there were no words. Tomek's grip tightened and he gagged again. A second later, he was on the floor, half breathing, half coughing.

Tomek stood over him. Olivier's eyes tried to focus on the polished leather of Tomek's black army boots. He ran his hands over his face making sure the tears that were forming in his eyes developed no further, then he looked up.

"Get two of the brats. We've got business in Marseille."

"What?" Olivier's eyes widened.

"You 'eard." Tomek walked away. "Leave Fierce Brat here and bring the other two." He stood at one side of the metal chest. "Let's get this in the van, and then you can bring the mopeds in 'ere til we get back."

Olivier struggled to his feet. "But I…" He frowned, at a loss for words.

"What?"

Olivier shook his head. "I…" Mouth open, but his mind could not seem to form the words he needed.

"You look like a dead fish. Now move, dumb'ead." Tomek kicked the metal chest to underline his order.

Olivier pulled his coat straight and complied.

voice recording

This is Jacques Forêt. I'm representing the parents of Pierre Mancelle.

> Are you police?

No. I'm a private investigator.

> Oh, I get it. You work for the police.

No. I work for Monsieur and Madame Mancelle who have engaged me to negotiate the return of their son, Pierre. Do you know where Pierre is?

> Yes. But I want my money.

And I want to see the boy. There's no money without my having sight of the boy so that I can see that he's alright.

> I'll get a picture and send it.

No. I want to see him for myself.

> …

Allo. Did you hear what I said?

> …Yes. I heard.

When can I see Pierre… If I can see Pierre you can have your money.

> I can let you talk to him.

I don't want to talk to him. I want to see him.

> I can give him this phone and you can ask him anything.

No! No talking on the phone. I want to see him for myself. There's no money unless I see the boy.

> ...

Allo... Allo?

> Do you know Séjalan?

Yes, I know it.

> Come up the *chemin* from *avenue* Tarn. Wait at the top. By the bench. 16.00.

No, that's too soon. We need time to get the money together. 19.30.

> No police or the boy dies.

No police. Just me. You have my word.

> And the money.

Yes. I will have the money and I will tell you where the money is when I see the boy.

> ... No. I get the money and then you get the brat.

No Pierre. No money. The boy first.

> ...

No Pierre. No money.

                        OK. I'll bring him. Séjalan, 19.30.

I'll be there.

thursday, september 20th, 11.49

The police officer moved the mouse and clicked the arrow button on the screen to halt the recording.

"No, I'd like to hear it again, please," said Pelletier.

The officer clicked the play button and the recording recommenced. Jacques, Didier and Pelletier listened in silence.

"Comparing your voice and his, Jacques, he sounds younger than you," said Pelletier.

Jacques nodded. "I'd guess twenties. Maybe early twenties."

"And he sounds local," added Didier.

"We'll get the recoding enhanced anyway but do you recollect hearing anything in the background that might help us?"

"I'm certain he was outside. But if it was a street, it was a very quiet one. There were no cars passing. There were no other voices, so not a *café*, a bistro or a bar." His phone rang. Jacques checked the number on the display. "That can wait," he said and switched his phone onto silent. "His knowledge of Mende also suggests that he is local, Bruno. If I were going to choose anywhere in this town to stage an exchange of this nature, that's exactly where I would go."

Pelletier nodded. "Right on the outskirts of town. Not much traffic and no-one likely to be there after dark."

"It's also quite open. So nowhere to hide."

"The investigation team can handle that, Jacques. I presume you will want to undertake the exchange yourself."

"Of course. Whilst the kidnapper doesn't know me, as far as I'm aware, Pierre does and he will be looking for someone he recognises. Are you planning to have Marie waiting out of sight but somewhere nearby?"

Bruno breathed deeply. "Ah, Madame Mancelle." He removed his spectacles and placed them on his desk and searched his pockets for his handkerchief. "I think it would be best for Madame Mancelle to know as little as possible. But the extent to which she is informed of the operation to recover Pierre will be a decision for the senior police officer in charge. My personal preference would be for her to remain safely at home and unaware until the operation is complete."

"Will a female officer by assigned to stay with her during the operation?"

"I will ensure that suggestion is considered. You will wear a wire and a vest, Jacques. Is that clear?"

"Of course."

Pelletier replaced his spectacles. He checked his watch. "We will reconvene at 17.30."

"What about fingerprints on the ransom note, Bruno?"

"We might be lucky, Jacques. We're waiting for the results."

***

Out on the street Jacques and Didier walked briskly back to the Vaux building.

"Some more work for you, Didier, in relation to Daniel St-Jean. His *maman* says she hasn't seen or heard from her son for six months. The last known address for the father and Daniel is in St-Étienne," said Jacques.

"Are you thinking Daniel St-Jean might be connected to the kidnapping in some way?"

"He might be, Didier, but he won't be working alone. According to his mother, he's not especially bright, and when you take into account his age, his wilfulness, it becomes more unlikely that he is working alone. But under the influence of his father, for example, he may not baulk at getting involved in something like this out of spite. Marie did remove one of his favourite targets and bullies need their subjugates. When you also take into account the amateur nature of the ransom note, it is possible that someone who had a previous connection with Pierre is behind all of this."

"What's the last known address?"

As they waited for the lights to change at the crossing on *boulevard* Roussel Jacques fished out a scrap of paper from his notebook.

"That's it," he said handing the note to Didier. We need to check current occupants, current owners if different and names of anyone who has lived there in the last six months."

"I know where this is, and it's not a good area of the city," said Didier as he glanced at the piece of paper. "I'll check registers of voters, et cetera, as usual."

thursday, september 20th, 13.07

Charles de Gaulle airport to the north of Paris was busier than expected. Delacroix made his way to the arrivals hall and immediately checked the information board. The flight from Dubai had landed on time. Now he just had to wait. He fully expected that an American travelling on a US passport and coming from the Middle East would be subject to a thorough check at immigration control. A stream of people, baggage in tow, began to flood the area. Delacroix scanned the travellers as they moved past him. Looking further back along the line, Delacroix spotted his associate. Tall, tanned and wearing a panama hat and pale grey suit, Wes looked every bit the important businessman. Delacroix waved and Wes acknowledged his presence.

As Wes reached Delacroix, the two men shook hands but remained silent. Delacroix led the way back to where he had parked his car. In the privacy of his vehicle they both employed their native North American English.

"You're looking well, Wes. Good flight?"

"Thanks. Yeah, just wish it had been shorter."

Delacroix pulled out onto the route des Badauds, heading west, and began to pick up speed. He stuck to the side roads until he was clear of the airport complex and headed towards the N104, his preferred type of highway for travel. The motorways were too heavily watched and had too many cameras for him to feel comfortable using them. Checking his mirror, he indicated and moved onto the short slip road. A few moments later he joined the traffic heading west on the *route nationale*. Delacroix relaxed back into his seat.

"We're heading to Verdon-le-Grand. That's where the new property is. We've got about an hour before we reach there and we can talk freely," he said.

"OK, so your plan of action for the property is what?" Wes looked out of the window at the passing scrub, bushes and trees.

"The most immediate issue is the roof. I've effected a temporary repair to make the place watertight but a roofer is coming first thing next week to size up the job and provide an estimate for the work." Delacroix glanced in the rear view mirror. "The plans for the refit for the interior of the property are in my briefcase in the trunk of the car. You'll need to contact our usual builders and get them booked to do the work as soon as possible. I need you to oversee all the changes. Getting the property in shape, Wes, is your number one priority." Delacroix paused as he concentrated on the bunching traffic.

In the silence Wes pulled out his phone and tapped out some notes. "So, what kind of town is this Verdon… whatever it's called?"

"Verdon-le-Grand," said Delacroix making a point of the appropriate pronunciation. "It's a small provincial town but there is a decent hotel which is at the end of the street and is convenient for the property. I wouldn't recommend staying there for the duration, though. Take a few days, a week at most and find yourself somewhere to rent close by. That way you can come and go unnoticed."

"And are you planning on staying much longer?"

"No, I've got other business in Marseille, and I'll be settling my room bill this evening and leaving early tomorrow morning. But the hotel is a good base to work from."

"What name are you using at the hotel?"

"John Oppenheimer. They think I'm an American tourist in the area looking for war graves and researching my family tree."

"Neat cover, man. So, I've gotta oversee the building works. What else have you got set up for me? There's gotta be something more interesting than managing a property renovation."

"There is and so far not that much already in place. Your extensive talents ain't gonna be wasted here."

Delacroix looked across at Wes, a wide smile on his face, that for once, reached his eyes.

"OK," continued Delacroix. "I'd like you to establish and put in place the supply chain. Verdon sits on the river Seine. The property is a fifteen minute walk from the river and the wharves and I've got a tame bargee on the payroll who will transport our goods for us, no questions asked."

"And the local mafia?"

"There ain't one in the way you mean. This is smallville, but there are some people you need to keep on the right side. I'll give you their contact details when we get back."

"Sure. And once I've got the necessary workmen in place I guess I'll just be overseeing the changes to the property, is that it?"

"Yeah, initially." Delacroix manoeuvred to get past a tractor before continuing. "I'll need you to make appropriate local contacts and to manage and work closely with our tame bargee. We can't have any slip ups with the transportation of goods."

"And your plans for introducing him to me?"

"We're all having dinner on his boat tonight."

"OK."

"As soon as the work on the property is progressing well, it would be good if you could start planning the jobs we need to undertake. First hit will be the museum in Le Cateau. It's a small town just over 200Ks from Verdon. It's about a three-hour drive along roads like this. Conveniently far enough away for any connection to us not to be obvious, but close enough for you to do all the ground work."

"And the goods this time?"

"Small works of…" Delacroix slowed and negotiated a roundabout. "…art. Mostly sketches but half a dozen small paintings too. All of them will fetch prices between €10,000 and €30,000 each. It's the small Herbin that we're taking from Le Cateau and we're leaving the Matisse. As nice as it would be to have a few of those going through our hands, they just attract too much attention."

"Do we have buyers or do I need to find them?"

"Already got some interest and they are mostly buyers you're already used to dealing with."

"OK. That's good to know."

"You should also plan for, and execute, the job in Saintes. We need to be running those two pieces of work almost simultaneously. Saintes is a larger town about 500Ks from here. You can do that journey in around six hours. Again, it's far enough away for our involvement not to be obvious. You'll have to be careful about how you manage your time on that job because of the distance. If you're going to use hotels make sure it's never the same one twice in succession."

"Got that."

"From Saintes we're taking the Courbet. Again, small items for which I have two buyers. The third job is in Rouen. The house in Verdon is too close for comfort to use as a base. From the *musée des Beaux-Arts* in Rouen we will be taking small items created by Braque. So you must plan and execute the jobs in Saintes and Le Cateau, remove yourself and then work on the job in Rouen. I'm exploring the acquisition of a property in Fougères for the third heist. That will give us a safe distance of just short of 300Ks. Hope your French is up to the mark, because you'll be working wholly in that language from here on."

Wes grinned. "That won't be a problem."

Delacroix glanced across at his passenger. "This really is smallville, Wes, and you must remember that. What you can get away with in Canada and the States, just won't cut it over here. OK?"

"Hey, don't fret. I've got it. You can trust me."

"Good to know. When we get to Verdon I'll drop you at the station which is on the north side of the town. You can pick up a taxi there and you need to ask for the hotel Belle Vue. It's about a five- or six-minute ride. I'm going straight to the property once I've dropped you off. After you've checked in at the hotel come to the house. It's number 38.

Then I'll take you through the changes to the interior and let you have the details for the heists. At the hotel I think it will be best if the staff believe that we don't know each other."

"Got that."

Delacroix lapsed into silence as he accelerated down the almost empty road. Nothing more was said for the final leg of the journey.

thursday september 20th, 14.35

The van began to roll through the outer suburbs of the city. Pierre and his fellow slave, Stupid Brat, were still asleep in the back. The lights at a junction ahead changed and Tomek pulled up sharply. The jolt woke Pierre. From his position behind the passenger's seat the boy could see the tops of the buildings along the street through the metal grill. The tarpaulin was only fixed in place behind the drivers seat. He stretched and heaved himself upright against the side of the vehicle.

"Sit still." Tomek flashed Olivier an angry glance as he turned towards his associate. "Yer bloody knee's bouncing again."

Olivier slid forward in his seat and put his right foot up on the dashboard. He let the window halfway down.

A fresh breeze blew in, and as Pierre took a deep breath he realised that the air had changed. Tomek shifted into first and the van began to move again. They crossed the junction and continued on. The sounds of traffic surrounded them, car engines, hooters, one driver shouting at another, and in the distance the sound of police sirens. They came to a halt again.

Pierre positioned himself against the side of the van so that he could look up, and out of the front window through the grill. The building on his left was old and of a yellowish stone. The windows were long and narrow and had ornamental ironwork across the front painted a dark grey. As he looked up further he saw the supports for the next storey had stone scrolls at the top. There was something familiar about the look of the building.

The van moved off again but at a slower pace. Tomek

cursed the traffic. Another building, this time grey stone with ironwork balconies and ornate finials on the supports. The next sound was the hoot of a different kind of vehicle, followed by the gentle increasing whir and hum of an engine and the dull clack of wheels on metal. *Metal on the road.* Pierre frowned.

He stretched as much as he could to see more, searching for something, anything that might confirm for him their location. *That was a tram. I'm sure that was a tram.* More traffic lights and they stopped. Another tram glided past and in the distance Pierre heard the rhythmic beat of Arabic drums. He stretched out his foot to nudge his fellow slave awake, but the boy just rolled away and curled up on his side. Pierre persisted until the boy glared at him, a scowl on his face. Pierre held his finger to his lips to silence him.

"I know where we are," he mouthed. The other boy shrugged and turned away again. Pierre reached across and tapped him on the shoulder.

"I know where we are," he mouthed very slowly and deliberately. The boy sat up and was about to speak but Pierre shook his head.

The van pulled up yet again and waited at a junction. Pierre checked out of the window and smiled. *That's St Vincent.* Turning to his companion, he nodded. As the van pulled away Tomek took a right and proceeded down a narrow street and then took a left. Pierre strained to see as much as he could as the vehicle threaded its way across the city. *This is the first. We're in the first.* He wanted to shout it out. He put both his hands across his mouth to stop himself saying anything. Pierre sat up. *I need to remember everything.* He took in a deep breath. *The sea. I can smell the sea.* The sounds of traffic were now accompanied by the clink of rigging in the wind. He knew they were crossing in front of the *Vieux Port*. Sitting forward, he drew a map on the floor of the van with his fingers. *We turned this way.* One hand pointing left. *And then this way.* His other hand pointed right. *So this must be Quai Neuve.* He nodded to his companion.

For the next few minutes the van turned and turned as Tomek wove his way through the cramped and shady streets. When Pierre next looked out of the window he didn't recognise anything. The buildings were tall, the shutters mostly closed, the streets constricted. Finally, the van pulled up. Tomek scrunched the gears and the van began to reverse very slowly.

"Get the brats out," said Tomek.

Olivier jumped out, unlocked the back door and, grabbing each of the boys by the arm, dragged them out onto a narrow and cobbled side street. They were frog-marched a few steps down a curving road, one car width across and under an arch that was the entrance to a tiny courtyard behind a tenement block. The building was surrounded by scaffolding and heavy plastic sheeting that reached from the ground up to the first floor. Olivier pushed them against the wall of the arch.

"Sit there and don't move."

They both slid to the ground. Pierre watched as Olivier took out his phone and moved the two steps needed so that he could stand at the entrance to the archway. He put his phone to his ear. Pierre wrapped his arms around his legs and wondered where Tomek might be. Not far away, he thought.

Olivier leaned back against the wall of the arch. His gaze shifted from the street, to him and Stupid Brat and back to the street again every couple of seconds or so.

Tomek appeared, glaring at him, and Pierre felt a shiver travel down his spine.

"You know what to do," Tomek said, shifting his attention to Olivier. "I'll be at my usual table outside Bar 55 in the square." And he strode down the street.

Pierre looked around. The tenement building was six storeys high. He'd counted the windows. Whilst he waited, he counted them again. The street was in shade as a result of the tall buildings either side but it gave no respite from the warmth of the late afternoon sun. With his head resting against the wall Pierre tried to gather his thoughts.

"Stupid Brat," commanded Olivier. "Man black jeans."

Olivier gave the boy the packet and pulled his gun part way out of his pocket. The boy darted out of the arch, handed over the drugs and darted back.

"You." Olivier held out a packet of drugs for Pierre. "Man, blue jacket and jeans."

Pierre delivered the drugs and the whispered message that he had decided on. As soon as he was back on the ground in the archway another order came in over the phone.

"Stupid Brat," he shouted. "Blonde, green dress." He pointed down the incline and passed the boy a small bag of pills.

"New Brat, black hair, pink jeans."

Pierre was on his feet and out of the arch. The customer was approaching, the boy took two running strides, handed over the package, whispered his message and dashed back. As he looked over his shoulder he just caught sight of the woman stashing her prize in the back pocket of her jeans. She walked down the street and into the sunshine. Pierre dropped down onto the floor just as his counterpart responded to another command from Olivier. No sooner had Stupid Brat returned to sit beside Pierre than Olivier spoke again.

"New Brat." Pierre jumped up. "Man, black hair, white shirt and grey suit." Olivier slipped the package into his hand. "No monkey business," he added in a snarl.

Pierre took the package, darted down the incline, delivered his message along with the packet and ran back.

"Stupid Brat."

For the next half hour or more the orders came unrelentingly. Neither of the boys had time to talk. As one returned the other was already up and running. The sun was at its height and the temperature was in the high twenties. Pierre could feel the perspiration on his forehead. The acrid odour emanating from his fellow slave's creased and soiled clothes was growing in intensity as the afternoon wore on. Pierre was also keeping count. *Twenty-three messages.*

"Stupid Brat." Pierre glanced over for a second. The boy looked tired and hot. Gradually he got up again.
We can get out of this. I know we can.

thursday september 20th, 16.12

In Verdon-le-Grand, on *rue des Déportés Martyrs*, Monsieur Archambault Hervé was in his armchair by the window. His head lay back against the antimacassar edged with lace that had been created more than forty years before by his wife. His breathing was shallow and steady but interrupted, every sixth or seventh time or so, by a longer, deeper breath accompanied by a light snore. The late 19th century mantel clock, his grandfather's winnings in a long running game of poker, ticked steadily on the dresser. Apart from the clock and Monsieur, the house was silent and cool in the late afternoon sunshine that beat against the shuttered windows at the back.

The quiet was barely disturbed by a key being pushed into the lock on the front door and carefully turned until the latch clicked back. Archambault's daughter-in-law, Sylvie, let herself in.

"Shush," she said to her five-year old grandson. "*Pépé* will be asleep."

Little Roland knew the routine and he put his forefinger to his lips and kept it there. The child stood back holding the door open so that Sylvie could walk through with her bags of shopping. Once deposited in the short hallway she returned to the doorstep to retrieve the potted plant she had bought for her elderly relative. As she stood up straight, the plant in her hand, she noticed the black car at number 38 again. She checked the number plate, but didn't recognise it. She looked the car over once more. Although it looked familiar, she couldn't be sure if it was the car from the previous day or not. She turned and went in.

"*Papa* will know," she whispered to herself. With the

plant safely placed on the small hall table, she quietly closed the door and led Roland through the house to the kitchen, unlocked the back door and ushered the boy out into the small garden.

Free at last from the rigour of school and shopping and walking with granny, Roland made straight for the sand pit. His favourite toy, a small aeroplane, was out of his shorts pocket and being dive-bombed onto an imaginary northern beach within moments. Sylvie smiled to herself as she recalled her own son playing in the pit when he was the same age as Roland.

Dragging herself away from the merging of past and present, Sylvie went straight to the kettle that was still full from when she had left earlier and switched it on. A cup, a glass and two saucers she had previously set out on a tray were joined by some milk from the fridge for her own tea and sugar from the cupboard. From the fruit bowl she took a lemon, cut it in half and sliced two generous rounds from the middle. The remainder she put in a small box, which she slotted onto a shelf in the fridge. With the tea made she carried the tray through to the main room at the front and placed it on the small dining table.

"*Papa*." The old man snored in response. "*Papa*," she said a little more loudly. Archambault stirred and eventually opened an eye. "*Papa*, it's Sylvie. I'm back from shopping and I've made us some tea."

"Sylvie? Yes. Tea, yes, tea with lemon, please." The old man frowned. "Tea? But I haven't had my lunch."

"Yes, you have, *papa*. I cooked lunch here and we had it together. Don't you remember?"

She handed him the tea. Archambault's expression slackened. His eyes darted from the glass on the saucer to Sylvie and then around the room. Sylvie placed the tea on the occasional table and sat on a dining chair facing him. She tapped his knee to get his attention and waited until he was looking at her directly.

"*Papa*, it's Sylvie. Your son's wife. I was here with you this morning. Now it's after school and your great-grandson is in the garden." She watched as the confusion on his face began to clear. A trace of the vacant expression in his eyes remained. "Have some tea," she said, nudging the saucer a little closer.

"Tea. Yes. Thank you." His voice was stronger when he spoke. He reached out, lifted the glass and took a couple of sips. He grimaced. "You've forgotten my sugar."

Sylvie smiled. "Perhaps, but at least I know you are back with me, *papa*." She added two spoonfuls to the glass and stirred it for him. Noticing that the old man's notebook had slipped onto the floor, she picked it up and handed it to him.

"*Papa*, the car yesterday at number 38, did you make a note about it?"

"Number 38? You mean old Vauquelin's place?"

Sylvie nodded and sipped her own tea.

"I note everything down," he said dropping the notebook onto his knee. "My old sergeant told me to always note everything down. Mark of a good policeman, he always used to say." Archambault shakily replaced his glass of tea. He picked up his reading glasses from the table and started flicking through his notebook. Having found the page he wanted, he presented the book to her.

The handwriting was no longer as smooth and flowing as it used to be, but the intention within each note made was clear. As was the registration number of the car parked outside number 38. Sylvie got up and went to the window. She looked through the gauze and compared the number in the notebook with that on the back of the car.

"Yes, it is the same car." Just as she was about to move away she saw a tall man on the opposite side of the street. Standing aside, she asked, "Is that the man from yesterday, *papa*?"

Archambault sat up and peered out, lifting the corner of the net. "Yes, that's him. Old Vauquelin. I told you he'd be back."

thursday, september 20th, 16.47

Strolling down *rue des Déportés Martyrs* in the late afternoon sunshine, Wes had no idea he had already become a person of note. His bags safely placed in his hotel room and the suit he'd been wearing on his journey deposited with the hotel dry cleaning service, he felt refreshed. He decided he would take a look around the place at the weekend. At number 38 he knocked on the door.

"Wes, you made it," said Delacroix. "Through here." He led the way into the principal room. "We've got all the comforts of home." He grinned as he gestured to the small foldable table and two camping chairs set in the centre of the room. On the floor by one of the chairs stood a bottle of rye, two crystal glasses and a briefcase. Wes sat in the free chair and glanced around the place whilst his associate poured them each a drink.

"Here's to another year of good business," said Wes as he clinked his glass against Delacroix's.

"Business. Yeah, let's get to it." Delacroix flipped open the top of his briefcase, lifted out a hefty folder and slipped out the contents onto the table.

"I've secured detailed plans for the galleries in Saintes and Le Cateau. Neither of them is going to be easy to access as they are both surrounded by other buildings. I'm still working on the plans for the museum in Rouen. The list of items that we need is here." He handed three sheets of paper stapled together to Wes. "Take your time looking over the list and become familiar with the items and their individual locations within each of the galleries. Some of the works are in the store room and not on display."

"That's going to make the planning more complex."

"You masterminded that bullion job ten years ago, Wes. I'm confident you can handle this. But we need to keep personnel involved down to the minimum and restricted to only people we already know and trust." Delacroix knocked back a good slug of his drink.

"And my up-front funding? There are gonna be some expenses for this." Wes swirled his drink around in the bottom of the glass.

"Bank account, credit cards, etc, in the name of Guy Vauquelin with €200,000 already deposited in a safe offshore account." Delacroix slid a brown envelope across the table. "Details in there along with a passport in the same name."

"And for how long am I expected to inhabit that new identity?"

"For as long as it takes."

"What have we got on the security systems in place in both of the buildings in the first two towns?"

"Those details are with the plans."

Delacroix sat back and poured himself another drink. He offered the bottle to Wes who shook his head and drained his glass.

"I guess you'll want that back," Wes said, reaching across and putting the glass down in front of Delacroix. "Be good if you could leave me the bottle, though."

"No problem." He moved the bottle across the floor to sit near Wes' chair. "One very important thing, Wes. All three of these jobs must be planned and executed with no weapons at all. Violence is not to feature at any point. The use of violence draws attention to the job and to me." Delacroix stared his companion in eye. "Clear?"

"Crystal. And if I do need to put pressure on someone?"

"You come to me. Everyone has their price and something they wouldn't want made public. It's just a question of finding out what both of those are. That's where my talents lie."

"OK."

"The plans for the changes to this property are in this

envelope. I need you to get the changes in motion as soon as. You'll see from the plans that we're re-wiring and upgrading, refitting the kitchen, the heating and hot water system. The *décor* needs to be tasteful and modern so that it can be sold as an ideal property for renting out as a first home on the property ladder. The roof space needs to be remodelled to the same modern spec. Once the work here is done, use this as your base and live here but the property must go on the market the minute the heists are complete and you've left. I can manage the subsequent sale remotely."

"And by that you mean I pack up all my stuff and send it ahead to the property we'll be using for the Rouen job before the heists take place."

"You've got it exactly right." Delacroix checked his watch. "If these three jobs go well, there could be more. I'm already looking at other small galleries in Bourg and La Rochelle."

Wes nodded.

"I need to go," said Delacroix. "Stay here as long as you like but we're meeting the bargee at 19.00 for *aperitifs* on his boat. It would be best if we arrive there separately." Delacroix closed his briefcase and snapped the catches shut. Going into the kitchen, he tipped some bottled water in each glass and rinsed them out. The glasses went into their holders in a small hamper on the draining board, which he also closed and fastened.

Back in the main room he tossed a bunch of keys on the table. "You own those now. I'll be leaving at 5.00 tomorrow morning, as I want to get back to the village as early as possible in the afternoon. Then I'll be in Marseille at the weekend. If you need to contact me use the usual number."

"OK and thanks. And don't forget to have some fun in Marseille. All business makes Ricky a very dull boy!"

Delacroix grinned. "Yeah right! Just for your information, there will be some fun. I've been promised some extra special sport," he said with a wink. A wide grin across his face, Delacroix made his way out to the car.

***

At number 37, Archambault sat in his chair, watching and waiting patiently. Sylvie was putting the final finishing touches to the neatness that she always insisted upon in the old man's kitchen when she heard him call her. She hurried through to the front room.

"He's back," he said as she came into the room and stood at the window. "Old Vauquelin, I told you he'd be back."

Through the gauze she saw a man at the boot of the black car. She watched as he stowed a hamper and a briefcase and then closed the lid. "But that…" She continued to watch as he moved around the vehicle and got into the driver's seat. It wasn't until she saw the hardtop on the car opening that she realised it was a convertible. He drove off further down the street.

"He always does that. Everyone does. He'll turn around in the entrance at the end."

"And you're sure that's the man from yesterday, *papa*?"

The car came past number 37 and Archambault lifted the corner of the net. "Yes. That's him."

She could see from the look on his face that the old man was adamant.

"But that's not the man we saw earlier," she said to herself as she walked out to the kitchen and then into the small garden. "Roland, come, it's time for you to go home, *chéri*."

thursday september 20th, 19.28

At the top of the *chemin*, Jacques waited. He checked his watch for the fourth time. *One minute to go.* Through his earpiece he heard the senior officer confirm that all personnel were in place. Jacques knew he was well protected. There were two armed police officers immediately behind the wall. A third was hidden behind a monument in the cemetery with a direct line of sight through the open entrance arch to where Jacques stood. He wanted to move. He felt like pacing but that would put him in danger and out of sight of the third officer. *Wait it out. I've just got to wait it out.*

"Red car approaching… Car now stationary." The message from the parked, unmarked police car further down the street came through his ear-piece. Jacques waited. He looked to his left. The pale grey holdall that looked like it contained the money, was sat on the tarmac just inside the entrance arch. Tomo, or whatever his real name was, would be walking into a well-planned trap.

"Not our mark," came the message in Jacques' earpiece.

"Damn it!" He stepped back and slumped down on the bench.

In response to another message in his earpiece from the officer in the graveyard, he stood up immediately and stepped forward. Looking left, he checked he was in the right line of sight and got a confirmatory message.

Jacques checked his watch again. *One minute forty seconds late.*

"Come on! Where are you?" The urge to pace was almost overwhelming but he fought it. He flexed his hands and fingers. He hadn't realised his fists had been clenched so tight that the joints in his fingers were beginning to ache. He checked his watch again. *Two minutes ten seconds late.* "How long do we wait?"

"Just be patient, Jacques." That message came from the officer in charge. Jacques recognised his voice. *Pelletier was right. If this really is going to be a no-show it's better that Marie doesn't know.*

Jacques and the police continued to wait in silence.

thursday september 20th, 19.54

Inside the empty tenement block Pierre and his companion had been pushed down the stairs to a utility room with a sliding door. Tomek had brought some chain and a heavy padlock from the van to secure it. At one side of the space stood three large washing machines still wrapped and waiting to be fitted. Pierre sat on the concrete floor, leaning against the rough and dusty grey wall. The only light came from the narrow and frosted street level windows at the top of the wall on his left. His companion wandered over to the machines. A piece of plastic was sticking up from one of them and he started to pull at it.

Pierre frowned as he glanced around at his new surroundings. *Maybe the workmen will come and find us.* His thoughts became a jumble in his head. Snippets of conversations. Snatches of the city that he'd seen. *I know that church.* He closed his eyes trying to remember the sounds. *A tram. I'm sure that was a tram.* He looked at the other boy still mindlessly tugging at the plastic. *I need to find papa.* He watched him for moment or two longer, then Pierre decided to take his opportunity.

"What's your name?"

"Stupid Brat."

"No, I mean your real name."

"Benoît."

"I'm Pierre, and I know where we are," he whispered.

"So what does that matter? They won't let us go," said Benoît, coming over and sliding down the wall so that he sat next to Pierre.

"No, but we could run."

"Where to? We don't even know where we are." He

stretched his legs out in front of him.

"I know we're in Marseille."

"How?"

"Shh. My *papa* sings at the opera house. My parents have an apartment here where *papa* stays when he's working."

Benoît sat up. "Really?"

"Yes."

"Can we go there?"

"I just need to see a street name then I will know how far away we are from the apartment."

"Liar! You don't know where we are." Benoît crossed his arms and turned away.

"I just need a street name," said Pierre. "That's all."

"But Marseille's like Paris. It's a big city. You can't know it all."

"I know, but we came down Canebière. I know that street and *papa*'s apartment is in the 1st."

"Will he be there?"

Pierre thought for a moment, his face and eyes clouded. "No, I forgot he's in Lyon this week."

The boys fell back into a sullen silence. Pierre could feel the wetness at the back of his eyes. He leaned over and let himself down on the concrete floor. With his back to Benoît, his hands under his head as a pillow, he curled up and let the tears fall silently into the dust.

The clank of the metal chain and the sound of the sliding door jolted both boys awake. Olivier appeared in the doorway, a gun in his hand.

"Come on, we've got work to do." He slung the chain around his neck and kept the gun trained on the boys. Pierre glanced at Benoît who got up without acknowledging the look. Head down and shoulders slumped, the boy slowly made his way across the space to the door. He followed.

"No trouble," threatened Olivier, pressing the barrel of his gun into the back of Benoît's head. With his free hand he grabbed Pierre's upper arm and marched them up the stairs, out of the small entrance at the back and into the tiny courtyard behind the archway. The same archway they had used earlier. Pierre sank to the ground, Benoît beside him.

Olivier's phone rang and he picked up the call immediately. Pierre knew it must be Tomek. It was a specific ring tone. A ring tone that always got an immediate reaction from Olivier. He listened and responded monosyllabically when required.

Olivier turned and took a step into the narrow street and continued to talk on the phone.

"I just need a street name," whispered Pierre.

Benoît let out a gasp, mouth open he stared at him. "What!"

"Shhh! He always chooses you first," he whispered. "Look for a street name."

Olivier turned towards them and took up his previous position on the opposite side of the archway, alternately watching the street and the boys. His phone rang and he pointed to Benoît.

"Stupid Brat. Man, brown hair, grey jacket." The boy got up, collected the small package and ran two strides into the street and back.

"You, brunette, silver dress." Pierre was on his feet as the other boy returned. As soon as he stepped out on the street he looked up. A blue street sign but the curve in the road meant the angle wasn't right. He couldn't read the sign.

"Stupid Brat, man, blue shirt and jeans."

Benoît was running as Pierre was sitting down. In the moment he had to himself he determined to run further and faster and to keep delivering his message.

"New Brat, woman, black dress."

The orders came one after the other, just as they had earlier in the day.

Pierre was tired and hungry. When their work was complete, Olivier marched them to the van that had been reversed into the entrance to the street at the top of the incline. They were shoved in and Olivier slammed the doors shut. From the passenger seat he pulled the tarpaulin back into place.

"Wait," shouted Pierre into the dingy green shadow that surrounded them. "We're hungry." He heard the click of the lock as Olivier secured the vehicle. He banged on the back door. "Wait, please wait!"

A heavy thump on the side of the van silenced him. *Tomek.* He scrambled as far back in the van as he could. He braced himself against the back of the passenger seat. Eyes wide and staring, he watched the doors. All was silence.

When Pierre felt calmer, he moved across and sat next to Benoît. The boy turned away.

"We're in the 7th," whispered Pierre. "That's not far from the 1st."

"But they've both got their guns." Benoît's face crumpled into tears.

"But Tomek isn't here when we are. If we run, Olivier can't catch us both."

"So what do we do?"

"You run down the street and I'll run up. Tomek said there's a square. That means more streets. I'll know the way from there."

Benoît whimpered and put his head in his hands.

Pierre looked away.

thursday, september 20th, 21.18

Jacques arrived at the apartment in Mende with a heavy heart. The operation to recover Pierre had been a complete failure. As he walked into the *salon*, Thérèse was waiting for him. Within moments her hopeful expression had slipped to disappointment.

"Jacques?" Thérèse got up from the sofa and crossed the room towards him.

He shook his head. "It's not good news," he said pinching his finger and thumb across the bridge of his nose. His sister stood still where she was.

"And the child?"

"We don't know." Jacques slumped down on the sofa. "Where are Lucien and Beth?"

"Your son is asleep in his cot in your room, and Beth is sleeping too."

"How has she been today?"

"A little better, I think," said Thérèse. "I think I've convinced her that it is best for her to sleep at the same time as the baby. But I still haven't managed to persuade her to use the baby monitor," she said, pointing to the small white object sitting on the coffee table.

"If she's getting more sleep and feeling better…that's some progress."

"But what about Pierre?"

"We had everything prepared and we were at the meeting place before the appointed time but whoever has Pierre didn't show up." He got up and went to the kitchen for a glass and poured himself a large whisky.

"We waited for three-quarters of an hour after the agreed meeting time, but it was still a no-show," he said sitting on the edge of the sofa staring into the bottom of the glass.

"What happens now?"

"We keep searching. We keep watching and waiting."

"And the police? Will they keep searching, Jacques?"

He took a large gulp of the whisky. "They will be following their procedures, as always."

friday, september 21st, 07.18

Jacques walked into the general office at the Vaux building in Mende. Both Didier and Maxim were at their desks, working. He felt a lump rise in his throat. *I should have been here sooner.*

"You don't look happy, Jacques," said Didier.

"It was a no-show. Pierre is still missing." Jacques took the chair that still remained at the side of his colleague's desk. "The whole operation was a waste of time. However, I do have a name for us to follow up. Olivier Duchamp. His fingerprints were on the ransom note that was delivered to Marie. According to Bruno, when I spoke to him after the debrief at the police station, Duchamp is a small-time crook. He's got a record of minor offences but there is no known current address."

Didier nodded. "Hmm… That explains the amateurish ransom note. What about the phone number quoted?"

"The phone number was Pierre's. They ran a trace at the police station and came up with nothing."

"So that phone is switched off and probably got the sim removed too."

"As expected, Didier. The number that was used to call me was a burner phone. The police ran a trace on that and nothing, just confirmation that it was a pre-paid with no attendant purchaser details."

"Another dead end. Hopefully the police are still watching those numbers."

Jacques nodded. "Maxim, find out everything you can about Olivier Duchamp, please. He must have parents somewhere who might be able to help us. Didier, can you run that name past all of your old snouts? One of them might have come across him before. Also, anything they've heard about Duchamp in connection with Pierre's kidnapping might help."

"I'm on it," Didier said, picking up his jacket to leave the office. "And I think I'll try my old friend who practically lives at the bar on the old quay."

Jacques stood. "Anything new in response to the press conference?"

"Nothing yet but I have got a few lines of enquiry to follow up on. And Pierre's tablet, I've been through everything on there and I think the gaming handle that we found, Tomahawk571, really is just another kid who likes that game."

"And Tomo?"

"No emails from or to a Tomo. No emails to or from another person that signed off as Tomo. Nothing."

Jacques frowned. "So why would he have that name written on one of his comics?"

"Could it be for a phone call?"

"That's a possibility. Can you check that with Monsieur Mancelle, please? If Pierre's father was monitoring his social media pages he will also have been monitoring his phone."

Jacques moved to the door at the end. "I'll be in my office, and I have a meeting with Alain at 11.00 this morning to finalise the buy-out. Let me know anything you find between now and then."

He left the room and crossed the corridor to his own office. In the quiet, he dumped his bag on the desk and leaned against it. Arms folded, he ran his eyes over the white board noted with details and progress on all current cases. The Éluard case that Didier had been following was now marked as complete with only the payment of the invoice outstanding. The watching and noting brief for Richard Laurent Delacroix was shown as referred back to Jacques. He looked over his shoulder. The same but slightly slimmer file was sitting there awaiting his attention.

Two new cases had been added at the bottom. He would

look at those first to decide if he would accept the commissions. *But not until I've got some coffee.* He was still regretting that third large glass of whisky from the evening before.

In the corner of his office he switched on the coffee machine. Whilst that worked, he unpacked his bag, switched on his laptop and sifted through the post. With a large breakfast cup of steaming and very strong coffee in his hand, he returned to his desk and settled down to work.

The first new commission was from an insurance company in connection with the payment of substantial compensation. It would be mostly a watching and noting brief, supported or refuted by interviews with the neighbours, colleagues and friends of the potential recipient, as required. The second new case related to family law and a dispute over assets. He picked up the phone and was about to dial his colleague's number when Maxim walked through the door without knocking.

"Maxim?"

"It's Pierre," he said, shoving a piece of paper under Jacques' nose. "We've got a lead, and I think it might be a genuine one."

Jacques grabbed the paper. "When did this…" He glanced to the top of the message. "Yesterday at 20.14. Why didn't we know about this sooner?"

"That's not a message board that we own, Jacques, so I can't control the feedback in the same way that I can with our own message boards. That list always comes into my inbox at around 1 or 2 each morning."

He looked at the paper again. "OK. If this is genuine, then I can only think of one person who would say his 'Papa sings opera' to a complete stranger. Can we get in touch with this person…" He scanned the printout for details of the contributor. At the bottom of the message it said 'OperaLover'. "There's no name or phone number, damn it."

"No, but to leave a message he or she has to be a registered user of the message board. The name OperaLover will be the login name and that name will have a related email address."

"Can we find him or her?"

"I've done some searches across all the message boards we use and that username doesn't come up anywhere else. I've replied to the message privately and asked whoever it is to contact you direct on your mobile."

"Thanks, Maxim." Jacques took a long drink of his coffee. "Has this response come only to us or to the *police municipale* as well?"

"Only to us, as far as I know. That thread is the one I started as soon as we knew Pierre was missing. The *police municipale* may still have seen it if they are following my thread themselves and I wouldn't necessarily know that if they were using a handle."

"OK. It could be a lucky break, then."

"Should I pass the information onto the investigation team or Magistrate Pelletier?"

Jacques thought for a moment. "No. Not yet. I want to hear what he or she has to say when they make contact before we pass this on."

Maxim nodded.

"The two new cases," said Jacques. "Accept both commissions, please." He handed over the appropriate items of post. "And the Insurance Company commission, I've noted that for charging at our premium rate."

Maxim left, and Jacques fished his phone out of his jacket pocket and placed it beside his desk phone. He noticed the charge level was less than half and plugged it in.

"If this really is genuine," he said, holding the piece of paper that Maxim had left, "at least you were still alive yesterday evening."

With his elbows on the desk he scraped both of his hands across his face. *But where in Marseille and for how much longer?*

friday, september 21st, 08.36

Didier left the bar on the quay. The ex-prisoner he had just met had contributed very little to the enquiry. When shown a copy of a mug shot of Olivier Duchamp supplied by the police, he'd denied ever knowing him. When Didier had reminded his contact of previous incidents that had been swept under the carpet to prevent a further conviction, suddenly information was more forthcoming. No, he hadn't seen Olivier Duchamp recently, but he had spotted him a couple of months previously hanging around the old warehouses on the wharves. Being precise about which warehouse had cost Didier €20.

With nothing more to be gained, Didier had moved on to Badaroux to call on the man who always walked his dog past the school just as the children were leaving. He hoped he might want to talk on this occasion. Didier rang the bell and looked over the crumbling exterior of the narrow three-storey house. The door was answered by the man Didier had followed.

"I'm Didier Duclos, Monsieur," he said as he held out his card. "We ran into each other a couple of days ago in the woods near the school?"

"Yes, I remember." He tightened the cord on his dressing gown. "Why are you here?" The dog at his ankles released a deep-throated growl.

Didier glanced down. The animal was eyeing him closely. "I'm a private investigator working for Monsieur and Madame Mancelle and I'm talking to anyone who might have any information about the disappearance of their son."

"I don't know anything about that." He withdrew and

attempted to shut the door, but Didier was too quick for him. The dog snarled.

"But you walk your dog in the woods every day just as the children are leaving school, Monsieur Buhot." The man shot him a startled look. "It is Monsieur Louis Buhot, isn't it?"

"How do you know my name?" The colour drained from his face.

"A boy's life is at risk, Monsieur. I really just want to ask you a few questions, that's all. May I come in?" The man glanced at the card that Didier still held out for him to take. Pulling his spectacles from his dressing gown pocket, he put them on and scrutinised it. Finally, he accepted the card as though he were inviting a plague into his property.

"Very well," he said standing back. "Fifi, basket," he told the dog and waved his arm towards a small room at the back. The dog skittered across the old and uneven flagged floor. Closing the door behind Didier, he eased past him in the narrow hallway that was dominated by a flight of heavy wooden stairs. Monsieur Buhot started to climb to the first floor and Didier followed.

At the top of the stairs was a small landing with two doors leading into the other rooms. Another spiral set of stairs lead up to the third floor. Monsieur opened the first door on his right. The room stretched the length of the property and the back wall had large full-length windows that overlooked a small balcony and provided views of the opposite side of the Lot valley. It was a light and welcome contrast to the gloominess of the ground floor. Monsieur Buhot collected a cup and saucer from a large dresser at one side of the room and resumed his place at the breakfast table.

"Please sit. May I offer you some coffee?"

Didier accepted and took the indicated chair. Adding sugar to his coffee from the small porcelain bowl on the table, he made himself comfortable and pulled out his notebook.

"Monsieur Buhot, three days ago this boy was

encouraged away from, or forced to leave, his younger sister at his school." Didier placed a copy of the photograph that had been in all the newspapers on the pristine white cotton of the table cloth. "His last instruction to his sister was to wait for their *maman* to arrive. He then ran out into the playground and didn't return. Do you recognise the boy?"

Monsieur Buhot took a sip of coffee. "I recognise the boy from the newspapers but not from the school."

"But do you remember seeing Pierre outside the school three days ago?"

Monsieur Buhot popped the remaining piece of a *croissant* into his mouth. He shook his head.

"I don't remember seeing him," he said as he reached for the basket of bread and a ceramic pot containing jam. From the pattern Didier guessed it must be strawberry.

Didier picked up his coffee and held it in his hands as he glanced over the table and the dresser on his right. Compared with the dishevelled exterior of the property, the interior looked like something out of a museum with every item in exactly the right place.

"Your dog, Monsieur, she must get a lot of attention each day as you walk by the school."

Monsieur Buhot smiled. "She does, Monsieur Duclos, and we both love the children. You see…" A pained expression flickered onto his face for a second or two.

Didier waited.

"And that was what happened the other day," Monsieur Buhot continued. "I didn't see your boy because of the other children."

"The children who pet the dog, Monsieur. I presume you are friends of their parents or are known to their families."

Monsieur Buhot gave Didier a sidelong glance. "My family is…disparate. I don't see my grandchildren as often as I would like." He turned his attention to his breakfast.

"But what about the two young men on scooters? Do you remember seeing them?"

Monsieur Buhot stopped spreading the butter on his piece

of *baguette*. After a moment he continued. He took the lid off the pot of jam and spooned some onto his plate. When he began to add jam to the bread Didier prompted him.

"The young men on the scooters, are they there regularly?"

"Monsieur Duclos, I haven't forgotten, nor am I ignoring, your question. I'm forming my reply." He cut the bread in half. "Yes, I do remember seeing the two young men on their scooters. I try to avoid them as much as I can. One of them is often ill-mannered and demanding. Being distracted by the children and letting them pet Fi helps with that."

Didier frowned. "You said 'often', Monsieur. So you must have you seen them at the school before. How often?"

"You asked are they there regularly? I would say not. I've seen them twice this week but not since that young boy disappeared. They have been at the school before, but that was about a month ago."

Didier made a note. "The one that's 'ill-mannered and demanding'… That sounds like you've had difficulties with these two." Didier let the statement hang in the air.

Monsieur Buhot poured himself another cup of coffee and dabbed his mouth with his linen serviette. He added one spoon of sugar to his cup and lightly stirred it, the spoon chinking against the china as he moved it.

"The older one is the ill-mannered one. Throwing out unsavoury comments."

I knew there was something, thought Didier. He leaned forward in his chair, "What sort of comments?"

"The kind that no polite person would ever repeat." He slipped the final piece of bread into his mouth and swapped his plate for his coffee.

"Do you know their names?"

"I'm sorry, but I don't." Monsieur Buhot tasted his coffee and grimaced. "Lukewarm," he said as he rose from the table. "Is there anything else, Monsieur?"

"Can you describe them?"

Monsieur Buhot placed his cup and saucer on his dirty plate and picked up the empty breadbasket. "I'm sorry, but they always wear their helmets. So I can't describe them in the kind of detail that you would want. But I do know that the older one is probably Eastern European. French is certainly not his first language, in my opinion."

Didier wanted to ask more. From the bottom of the stairs he heard a single restrained bark and Monsieur Buhot smiled in response. He collected his notebook from the table and put it back in his jacket pocket.

"Thank you, Monsieur Buhot, and if you remember anything else please call me. The number is on my card." He stepped away. "And the ill-mannered young man on the scooter," he said turning to face his host. "If you need me to have words with him, just call me."

Monsieur Buhot immediately looked away. "That won't be necessary," he snapped.

Another single and slightly louder bark came from the hallway. "Fi needs her morning walk," he said, a bright smile appearing on his face.

friday, september 21st, 09.42

Jacques picked up his mobile for the twentieth time, hoping to see a missed call. Not that he would have missed the call anyway; his phone had been with him constantly. He just wanted OperaLover to ring. He closed the cover of the Delacroix file and pulled the note he had made whilst working through it towards himself. *I wonder…* As the thought took shape in his mind he picked up his mobile and went to his contacts list. He pulled up the number for the restaurant in Messandrierre. Picking up the desk phone, he dialled and hoped that Gaston was there.

"Gaston, *ça va*…No, no news of Pierre as yet but we're working hard to find him… Yes, I know… Yes, look I don't have much time and I have a couple of questions about Delacroix… I believe he eats regularly at the restaurant… Right and how does he pay?… Always?… On every single occasion?… I've seen him in the bar sometimes in the evening, how does he pay his bar tab?… I see… Thanks, Gaston… I don't know. Pierre has to be my priority… Yes, and thanks."

He put the phone down and looked at his note of dates and places. *I wonder, Monsieur Delacroix.*

Picking up his office phone again, he dialled Maxim's number and asked him to come through. In the meantime he re-read the list, tapping his desk with his forefinger as he did so.

"Ah, Maxim. I've been through the Delacroix file and there are some sightings that I would like us to focus on. I've also just spoken to Gaston at the restaurant in Messandrierre, and I would like us to handle the next level of enquiry in a particular way."

Maxim frowned. "How do you mean, Jacques?" Maxim liked being at his desk. He understood computers and he was comfortable with straightforward questions over the phone. He voiced his concerns. "Are you expecting me to follow him or something?"

Jacques shook his head and retrieved his note. "The sighting in Saintes just before Christmas last year. That correlates to a period where I've logged his absence for up to eight days. According to my notes he wasn't in Messandrierre that weekend when Beth and I arrived at the chalet. A few days later that week, I had lunch at the restaurant and he wasn't there then but he returned at the end of the ensuing weekend. We need to explore that. The same applies to the sighting in Bourges eight months ago, the sighting in Rouen six months ago and the sighting in Blois just over three months ago. In each of those instances he was missing for about a week."

"OK. So how do you want me to handle this?"

"Check hotels and rental accommodation in each of those towns and the surrounding areas but don't use his name. Just send them the photograph that we already have posted on all of our social media pages and the websites and forums—"

"I don't understand, Jacques. How is that going to help us?"

Jacques grinned. "I've seen Delacroix at the restaurant in Messandrierre and it occurred to me that we had never asked Marianne to go through her books and check for dates when he was there. I've just spoken to Gaston, and Monsieur Delacroix eats there a couple of times a week, most weeks. He never books in advance and he always pays in cash. When he is in the bar he also always pays in cash, either as he buys each drink or for his tab at the end of the evening."

Maxim shrugged. "Maybe he doesn't believe in credit cards or cheques."

"Perhaps, but cash is untraceable, a credit card isn't. He arrived when his uncle died," Jacques paused. "And I'm no longer sure about that family connection but I've no hard evidence. But he's been here for over two years, and he's never once used a credit card despite all his transactions in the village during that time. I find that unusual."

Maxim nodded. "Yes, I see what you mean. And when you think about the magazine that interviewed him a while ago, his business interests, he must have bank accounts, mustn't he?"

"Yes. So get that photo circulated and see what comes back. We'll talk again when we've got the results." Jacques handed over the file. "One more thing," he said as Maxim got up. "Can you check with the restaurant, please, and ask if he's ever explained or made mention of his absences to either Gaston or Marianne?"

Maxim nodded and just as he closed the door, Jacques' mobile rang. He checked the display. It wasn't anyone in his contact list. He picked up the call.

"*Allo*, Jacques Forêt speaking… Yes, that's right, and your name, Monsieur?… No, I'm not the police… I work for Monsieur and Madame Mancelle and no-one else, until we find their son, Pierre… I'd like to talk to you in person… No, anything we discuss will be in absolute confidence… Yes, I can be there and your name, Monsieur?… Thank you… Yes, this afternoon at around 14.30?"

Jacques ended the call and immediately saved the caller's number to his contacts list and typed in the name Christophe Renner, then he walked through to the general office.

Didier was at his desk, a dark questioning look on his face and Maxim was on the phone.

Jacques pulled a chair up to his colleague's desk. "Anything from your snout or Monsieur Buhot?"

"Not much from my contact. Last sighting of Olivier Duchamp was around some old warehouses on the old quays but nothing recent. I checked the wharf before I went out to Badaroux, there was no sign of the mopeds nor the white van that my snout mentioned. Monsieur Buhot, though. He's hiding something, Jacques. I just don't know what yet. He also says that one of the young men on scooters seen on the CCTV footage at the school is probably Eastern European. Monsieur has heard him speak and may be able to recognise his voice. This individual insulted Monsieur Buhot in some way. Again, he was very cagey about the details."

"Run a background check and see what comes up. Maxim has had a lead on Pierre from one of the message boards we use. I've spoken to the man who reported the sighting and I'm meeting him in Marseille this afternoon. Get the car, a change of clothes and meet me back here." He glanced at his watch. "10.30."

"What about your meeting with Alain?"

"It can wait, but I'll call him and reschedule." Jacques was on his feet, mobile in hand as he dialled Alain's office in the sister building across the road. *You're not going to like this.* He waited for Alain to pick up.

friday, september 21st, 14.03

From his table in the restaurant in Messandrierre, Richard Laurent Delacroix could see the mountain peaks shimmering in the afternoon sunshine. The seven-hour drive from Verdon-le-Grand had taken its toll and left him ravenous. Having eaten, he felt himself again and called to Gaston for the bill.

"Shall I book a table for you for later in the week?" Gaston slipped the small dish containing the bill onto the table.

"No, thanks," said Delacroix as he pulled his wallet out of his jacket pocket. "I'm not sure if I'll be around much this week." He dropped a €50 note onto the dish and Gaston picked it up. Lifting his jacket off the back of his chair, he followed Gaston to the bar to collect his change.

"Well, have a good trip," said Gaston, placing the notes and change on the counter.

Delacroix scooped it up. "Thanks, I will." Bundling the money into his trouser pocket, he slung his jacket over his shoulder and strolled out of the restaurant to his car. The final leg of the day's first journey was the few hundred metres from the restaurant to the farmhouse on the top road. As he drove the route he wondered about taking a couple of hours to get some sleep. Fighting back a yawn, he decided against it.

"Got too much to do. I can bed-down in the apartment in Marseille when I get there," he said as he took the final turn onto the short drive to his property. Moments later he was letting himself in. His jacket hung on the post at the bottom of the staircase he went back out to the car and collected his bags.

Kicking the front door shut, he dumped everything on the floor. The holdall that contained the clothes he'd use for his alter ego of Guy Vauquelin he took down to his working space in the basement, then he walked straight through into his *cave* and opened a locked door at the far end. This led to the wood-burning stove that ran the heating system throughout the house. He loaded some logs, added the clothes from the holdall, added some more logs and then set the stove going.

Returning to the *cave*, he unlocked the gun-cupboard and removed his hunting rifle and some ammunition. Some sport once the business was concluded would be a perfect end to the week.

Upstairs, he packed some clothes and refreshed his toilet bag. From his safe, he collected some cash, which he slotted into his wallet. Within an hour of returning home he was locking the front door. He checked his watch.

"Should be in the 7th around 19.00," he said as he got into the driver's seat of his black convertible and switched on the ignition.

friday, september 21st, 14.26

The *Vieux Port* area in the city of Marseille was noisy and busy. A cool breeze blew in from the sea, rattling and clattering the rigging on the numerous pleasure boats on the sound. The ferry from one quay to the other chugged backwards and forwards on its timed treadmill. A local police car, siren blaring and lights flashing, demanded a route through the traffic of the post-lunchtime return to work. Jacques and Didier walked down the *Quai Rive Neuve* looking for Bar de la Mer, opposite which was meant to be a bench. They kept walking.

"There," said Jacques, having spotted the sign for the bar. As they approached, the wooden bench on the opposite side of the road that ran around the perimeter of the port area came into view.

"And that's the bench," said Didier. "And it's empty." He strode out to make sure that he could get there before anyone else. Didier settled himself at one end of the bench and Jacques joined him at the other end a few moments later. Jacques checked his watch.

"Just a couple of minutes to wait," he said.

Didier scanned the marina. "I've often wondered about owning a boat," he said. "But my wife wasn't keen. She couldn't even swim."

Jacques smiled. *Yes, we all limit ourselves to some extent for the sake of marital harmony.* He kept his thought to himself.

"Maybe now is your opportunity," he suggested.

Didier shrugged. "Perhaps if I lived nearer the coast I might look into it."

"We have rivers and canals, Didier. They both take boats.

I don't think the coast is an absolute requirement to own a boat."

Didier stood, hands in his trouser pockets. "No. If was going to have a boat it would be something like that one over there," he said.

Jacques turned to look. Progressing through the outer harbour wall and into the central channel of the sound was a yacht under sail. A crew member was bringing down one sail and a second man was at the helm of the traditionally-built and rigged vessel. As she glided through the water tourists stopped to watch.

"That looks like a lot of money, Didier."

He nodded. "A lot of work too, but it would be worth it for the feel of the ocean and the wind."

Jacques looked at his colleague with a new understanding. "You've been on a boat like that before?"

"A tall ship, Jacques. A long time ago. I once crewed on a 19th-century schooner for the Tall Ships' race. 1968. Beautiful vessel, four masted, gaff rigged." He smiled to himself. "Just eighteen and had the time of my life!"

Jacques was surprised and impressed. They watched in silence as the yacht eased into a berth on the opposite side of the harbour.

Checking his watch, "He's late," said Jacques.

"I make it 14.31," said Didier. He turned to scan the tables in front of the restaurant, the passing tourists and local people looking for anyone who might be heading directly towards them.

Jacques followed suit.

"We can't afford for this to be another no-show." Jacques began to pace as he continued to scan the passers-by. He checked his watch again.

"Three minutes late, come on, Monsieur Renner. Come on." Jacques continued to pace. Didier settled himself back on the bench. Glancing across the harbour, he watched the yacht as it tied up.

Jacques' phone rang and he picked up the call.

"*Allo*, Jacques Forêt… No, that's my colleague, Didier

Duclos... No, he works for me. Anything you say to me can also be said to Didier... Yes, you have my word."

Jacques ended the call. "That was Renner," he said. "He'll be here in a moment." He began to scan the crowds of people again. Just as he said the words a man in his thirties in a blue business suit approached them from the side street behind.

"Christophe Renner," said the man as he held out his hand for Jacques to shake.

"Are you happy to talk here," asked Jacques as Renner moved across to greet Didier.

"Yes," he said and took a seat.

Didier unfolded the city map that he'd picked up from Tourist Office as they passed on their way from the car park to the harbour.

"Can you show us exactly where you saw Pierre?"

Renner took the map and placed it on the bench between himself and Didier.

"It was in the 7th," he said. He moved his finger across to the harbour and up the street he had just walked down. "Here," he said pointing at a small square about ten minutes' walk away. "This is where Bar 55 is. Castellane in the 6th is on this side, but the boy you're looking for was in this street here in the 7th." He indicated a narrow street that came off the square between two major roadways. "That's *rue des Licornes.*"

"And you're certain it was Pierre," asked Didier pulling the photo out and showing it to Renner.

"Yes, I'm certain," he said without even glancing at the picture.

"Can you just look at the photo, Monsieur, and confirm that, please?"

Renner looked down and nodded. "Yes, that's him."

"Can you take us through exactly what happened?"

Renner grimaced. "This is where things get a bit delicate," he said.

Jacques waited.

Renner cleared his throat. "I'm a great fan of opera,

Monsieur Forêt. I've heard Monsieur Mancelle sing here in our own opera house. He has a wonderfully mellow tone of voice and when I saw him in Bizet's *Les pêcheurs de perles*, last year, I thought it was the best thing he'd ever done. Anyway, when I want to immerse myself in the music at home I find…umm, a couple of pills helps."

That's what he's been so nervous about. Jacques had no interest in the man's questionable habits, nor would he make a judgement. He just wanted facts.

"These pills Monsieur, ecstasy?"

Renner nodded. "No one I work with knows. It would be frowned on."

"And you get these at Bar 55?"

Renner nodded.

"So how does Pierre fit into this?"

"He's one of the runners."

Jacques glanced across at Didier. This wasn't what he wanted to hear. *Pelletier and the investigation team were right all along.* Jacques stood and took a couple of steps away. *How did you get involved in this, Pierre?* He shook his head. Resuming his seat, he continued.

"How do you know when there is anything available to you?"

"A text message," said Renner.

"Have you still got the last one."

"I usually delete them as soon as I've read them," he said pulling out his phone to check. "Yes. I've deleted it."

The phone used to send the text will probably be another pre-paid, thought Jacques. He knew it was a long-shot but he decided he would ask the question anyway.

"What about a name for your supplier?"

Renner shrugged. I don't know the guy's name, honestly, I really don't know. But the texts are always signed off as Tomo. They just give a time, a place and Tomo. That's all I know."

"What about a description?"

"Erm… Not as tall as you, Monsieur Forêt, about 1.8 metres or so, muscular, dark hair, olive-skinned and probably Eastern European. Well, his looks suggest that."

Didier scribbled down the description. "You said Pierre was one of the runners, Monsieur. How many are there?"

"Two, I think."

"OK, so, how does this all work?" Didier, notebook still open, continued. "You get the text, you go to the bar, then what?"

Jacques had seen it all before, in Paris. But he let the question be answered.

"I was on my way back to the bank, which is in the 1st, after lunch. I called at Bar 55 and had a coffee. Tomo, or whatever his real name is, was sitting at his usual table. I paid for the coffee. Got up and as I made my way by his table I nodded and slipped the folded €20 note under the rim of the saucer at the edge of his table. He nodded and called his associate. I headed across the road and into *rue des Licornes*. It curves round and as I came round the bend the boy ran up to me and gave me the packet. And that's when he said, 'Papa sings opera'."

Jacques grinned. *He's a clever boy.*

"Did he say anything else?"

"No, just that. He took me completely by surprise. I couldn't do anything, I had to get back to the bank. I could hear someone else coming so I just looked the other way, headed down the street, along the main road and back to work."

"You said he had an associate," said Jacques. "Can you describe him?"

"Not really. I only caught a glimpse of him but he's always around when Tomo is."

"Anything you can tell us will be helpful," encouraged Didier.

"Dark coat. Might be dark green, or dark grey maybe. Dark blond hair, scruffy looking."

"Would you recognise him if you saw him again?"

"I'm not sure."

Jacques pulled out the photo of Olivier Duchamp and passed it to Renner. "Might that be him?"

"It's the coat I remember rather than his face. It was a warm afternoon and the coat seemed unnecessary. It might be him, but I can't be certain."

"Alright. One last thing, how did Pierre look to you?"

"Scruffy, and he had a black eye."

Jacques winced at the last piece of information.

"But no other injuries?"

"I only saw him for a second or two, Monsieur Duclos. The black eye couldn't be missed. Someone's given the poor kid a hefty thump."

Didier snapped his notebook shut. "Doesn't it bother you that children as young as nine years old are being exploited like this?"

Jacques wondered if he should say anything in response, but that would mean openly admitting he'd worked drugs cases before. It would also alert their informant to his previous occupation and he didn't want to rattle him. He left Monsieur Renner to defend himself.

"Despite what you see here, Monsieur Duclos," Renner gestured towards the harbour full of expensive boats of all shapes and sizes. "There's a lot of poverty in this city, especially in the *Quartiers Nords*. The runners are normally street kids and I've always thought that working for a pusher was probably only just a little better than living on the street."

And the local mafia make it easy for that to happen. Jacques was unmoved by Monsieur Renner's explanation. "Thanks for your help. We'll take it from here."

"But you won't reveal that your information came from me, will you?"

"You have my word, and the *police municipale* aren't really interested in users like you, Monsieur Renner. It's the dealers and suppliers they want."

"Thanks." Renner shook Jacques' hand. "And if you're interested, Tomo will probably be sticking around for the weekend trade."

Jacques nodded. "If you get another text please forward it on to my number."

He already knew what he was going to do next. Monsieur Renner left and Jacques opened the map and spread it out on the bench.

"From here, Bar 55 is up this street behind us, take a left and then first right then along this street here to the square. Let's take a look, Didier." Folding the map back so that only the area they were walking through was visible, he tucked it into his jacket pocket and set off at a brisk pace. Didier matching his stride, they threaded their way through the crowds around the port. The number of people began to thin a little the further away from the harbour as they progressed. On the wide street that led to the square, Jacques stopped and checked the map.

"There's a street here on the left that leads to another street that runs parallel to this. You continue on to the bar along here. I'll duck down there and approach the place from the opposite direction."

Didier nodded and strode off towards the square.

Jacques walked down the side street and took a right at the end. Striding out along the parallel thoroughfare, he took another turn at the end, and rounded the final corner into the square. Bar 55 was on his right. As he approached he saw Didier at a table in the corner of a marked out area on the street. From that point Jacques reasoned that his colleague would have a good view of anyone approaching from any one of three of the routes leading into the square. He took a table at his side of the marked out area from where he could observe the other routes leading in. The waiter approached and Jacques ordered a *café allongé*. As he waited he scrutinised the area centimetre by centimetre. He wanted to have a complete and accurate picture in his head. He could see the entrance to *rue des Licornes*. It was very narrow and the curvature was such that he surmised that the length of vision along that street would be very short.

"Ideal," murmured Jacques.

His drink delivered, he paid the waiter immediately. Alone again, he considered the position of each of the tables. He pulled out the map and laid it flat. *Renner would have been heading in that direction to get back to the bank.* He tapped the route on the map. *That table or that one.* He looked over to the opposite side of the marked out area. Both tables were at the perimeter of the outside seating area and both would have a view of potential customers approaching from the square and from inside the bar, and probably the best view of *rue des Licornes*.

His coffee finished, Jacques rose and nodded to Didier. He set off up the main thoroughfare heading north from the bar. The map indicated that *rue des Licornes* joined the main street, but he wanted to know exactly where. As he strode along, he discovered it was only one block and *rue des Licornes* came out onto another short side street. Jacques waited for Didier to catch up.

"Let's see what we've got," he said as they both entered *rue des Licornes*.

On the left stood a six-storey building surrounded by scaffolding which was partially covered with heavy plastic sheeting. At the back was a small archway and a small courtyard beyond. The courtyard was covered in debris from the now-halted renovation work.

Jacques and Didier investigated. The entrance at the back was boarded up and secured with a heavy padlock on a bar stretched across the middle. The windows for the first floor were out of reach without a ladder. Only the windows on the top floor and the one below had been renewed.

"Let's check the front and the other side," said Jacques, leading the way around the building. At the front there was no visible means of access. On the remaining fourth side, some of the plastic sheeting had been damaged and was flapping in the breeze. Jacques ducked under and looked up. There was only rendered wall with fire exits at alternate levels beginning with the first floor. The remains of the old ironwork for the original fire escapes were protruding from the sides of each doorway. All the doorways were boarded up.

"Very much a work in progress," said Jacques as he

emerged from the cover of plastic. "There's no sign of access here."

"If this building is being used then it must be the back entrance and they must have keys."

Jacques nodded. "And if they have keys, someone connected with this halted renovation is getting paid."

Didier nodded. "What do you want to do?"

"We'll find somewhere to stay and come back this evening and stake out Bar 55."

friday, september 21st, 20.54

Didier's car was parked on the opposite side of the square from Bar 55. Slouched down in the driver's seat, Didier had the rear-view mirror angled so that he could see what was happening on the terrace area.

Jacques was seated at a table in one corner reading a newspaper. A waiter breezed by and collected an empty coffee cup and saucer from his table.

"More coffee, Monsieur."

Jacques shook his head. "A small *pression*, please."

The waiter nodded and moved away. Jacques scanned the tables but nothing had changed. He glanced over at the car. Nothing had changed there either. The cars that had been parked on either side of Didier's vehicle for the last hour or so were still there. The waiter returned with the beer and a paper mat for the table, obscuring his view of the terrace for a few moments.

As soon as the waiter had gone Jacques checked the seating area, the parked cars and the street again. Along the main thoroughfare that ran eastwards from the square, heading towards him, Jacques spotted a man in army boots, black trousers and shirt. The man fitted the description given by Monsieur Renner.

"Possible sighting," Jacques whispered into his microphone.

"Got that," replied Didier.

Jacques watched. The man pulled a chair back from one of the two tables that he had identified as being the ones their mark might be using and took out his phone, placing it on the table. The waiter approached, hovered as he spoke to the customer and then returned inside the bar. Jacques was too far away to hear what had been said, but soon after, the waiter re-appeared and placed a coffee on the table. The bar was filling up. People were coming and going. The noise level was beginning to rise.

From behind his table, Jacques could hear someone approaching. As the individual moved level with him, he noticed it was a man, but he kept looking ahead. The man's stride was military and gave the illusion that he was taller than his 1.75m of actual height. His build was wiry and his gait demonstrated that his attitude to everything was assured. As he walked on, Jacques instinctively looked up. There was something about the walk; the hold of the shoulders and the close cropped medium brown hair that seemed familiar to him. The man took a seat at the table occupied by the individual he and Didier were watching. With his back towards him, Jacques couldn't be sure if he did recognise the second person or not. The newspaper positioned so that he could see over the top, Jacques waited for the newly-arrived person to look either left or right. A profile would enable him to decide. The waiter approached, and the man turned to his right.

Damn it. I wasn't expecting you.

"Didier, I need to get out of here. At the table with our mark is Gilles Fournier, my old boss." He rose and placed a note under the glass for the cost of the drink he had barely touched. Walking around the corner, he waited for Didier to join him. Jacques pulled out the city map and scanned it, looking for other vantage points to continue watching.

"We need to stay and keep an eye on them, Jacques," said Didier as he sprinted across the street. "They've just been joined by someone else." He held out his phone with a shot of the three men around the table.

Jacques looked at it and, stretching his finger and thumb across the photo, he zoomed in on the third man.

"Richard Laurent Delacroix," he said.

Jacques showed Didier the map. "If we cross here and take that back street and cut right here, we can come out on the main street here and access the top of *rue des Licornes*."

"Which will give us a good, but short sightline for that table."

"Get the car and I'll go on foot."

***

At the table in Bar 55, Richard Laurent Delacroix was being his most affable self. He took a long drink of the beer in front of him and moved the glass to one side.

"To business, gentlemen," he said, pulling some stapled pieces of paper from the inside of his jacket pocket. "I'm having a few problems with the numbers." He looked from one to the other. Tomek crossed his arms and leaned back in his chair. Fournier's dark beady eyes moved steadily from Delacroix to Tomek and back again.

"Let me show you what I mean," he said smoothing out the papers he held. "Over the last three years, this graph shows the trend for the income from our products. If you compare the income from the last twelve months with that for the same period last year…" He flipped over to the next page. "You'll see a deficit. A three percent deficit."

Tomek remained motionless, but Fournier picked up the sheet and examined it closely.

"We have costs," he said. "And those are going up all the time."

"Good point," said Delacroix. "But I looked into this a little further and…" He flipped another sheet over. "I can tie this trend right back to late summer in 2009."

Delacroix drank the last of his beer and beckoned to the waiter. "Same again, is it?" When the waiter arrived at their table, he gave the order. The conversation paused until the waiter had returned with a tray full of drinks.

Turning the paper round so that the orientation was landscape, Delacroix finally continued. "Let's take a look at the details, shall we? Here, in January through to June, the income is steady and as expected," continued Delacroix. "In June we had a bit of hiatus, didn't we, Gilles?"

"As you know we had a key member of the supply chain disappear," said Fournier.

"Unfortunate, I know, but it prompted an official investigation and drew too much attention." Delacroix smiled at Fournier. "Just remind me of one thing," he said as he turned his attention to Tomek. "When was it exactly that you joined us?"

Tomek shrugged.

Delacroix supplied the answer. "Late autumn, 2009. So if we look at the income from late autumn onwards we can see that in January the following year, 2010, the income from our goods begins to gradually decrease. Not by much. Just half a percent. But then that half a percent deficit begins to grow until it becomes one per cent and then one and half and so on." Delacroix waited for an explanation.

"No ideas or explanations?" Delacroix watched Tomek who glanced at Fournier and then stared straight ahead. As nothing was forthcoming, he drained his beer and stood.

"I'm here for the whole of the weekend," he said. "I want the deficit made up plus a commission of five percent for the loss of income and I expect to be advised of how that will happen and when before I leave." Pocketing the papers, he moved away from the table and across the road.

As soon as Delacroix was out of earshot Fournier leaned across the table. "Wherever that money is, find it and be quick!"

Tomek glowered at Fournier. "I'm the fall guy. What a surprise?"

"It's no surprise to me. I know I haven't had my hands in the till."

"But yer not afraid to take back'anders, though, are yer?" Tomek drained his coffee and placed the cup on the saucer with a clatter.

"Just get that money," snarled Fournier. "And get rid of that idiot who runs the Brats. He's drawing too much attention. Just like you are with your sport."

"What do yer mean?"

"Your hunting, Tomek. It has to stop. That idiot you work with? Ask him about the ransom note." Fournier got up and left.

***

From the shadow in the lee of the tall buildings either side of the *rue des Licornes*, Jacques waited and watched. The man in black was still at the table vacated by Fournier and Delacroix, but he showed no sign of leaving. Jacques watched as his mark picked his phone up from the table and stared at it as though he couldn't decide if he wanted to make a call or not. After a few moments he put the phone to his ear.

Fifteen minutes later, he was on his feet and striding towards the *Vieux Port*. Jacques followed him through the back streets. He zig zagged across the 1st and along a narrow and steeply climbing side street. At the end, he took a left that brought him out at the foot of the steps that led into the central railway station.

Jacques hung back a little. *Looks like he's heading towards the Devereux brothers' territory.* As he reached the top of the steps the man turned towards his right and Jacques sprinted out from the corner of the building shielding him from sight. He took the steps two at a time. At the top he turned right and entered the station. His mark was striding ahead along the central concourse. Jacques followed him out onto the back streets behind. A few more turns and the man entered a nightclub. Jacques waited in the entrance of a closed shop door front. Dressed as he was and at his height, he knew he would draw too much attention if he went inside the club. In this area of the city, run by the Devereux brothers, he could guess what kind of clientele such a place would entertain.

He waited an hour, but his mark did not show himself. Jacques decided to call it a night. He texted Didier to let him know that he was returning to the hotel.

saturday, september 22nd, 06.00

In Verdon-le-Grand, Madame Sylvie Hervé walked into the hotel Belle Vue to begin the first of her weekend shifts. As usual, her colleague, Bernard the night porter, had left all the filing and tidying up for Sylvie to do. She often felt that the man considered her to be his personal administrative assistant. Sylvie always made sure, whenever she next saw Bernard, that he was fully aware of the inconvenience he had caused. Not that she had ever noticed any change in his behaviour as a result.

In the peace and quiet of the early morning Sylvie processed the key cards, noted the rooms to be cleaned and checked through the inbox for bookings, company messages and anything else that may need her attention.

She noted that an American in room 5 had checked out, a Frenchman in room 7 had checked in and that another new guest had checked in during the late afternoon on the day before yesterday.

With her reception desk in order and all the clutter left by Bernard tidied away, Sylvie made her way to the small kitchen area behind the reception desk to make herself some coffee.

As she returned to her post two of the cleaners arrived and they chatted briefly, her father-in-law's health and falling mental capacity always being a topic of conversation and concern.

Sylvie loved her part-time work at the hotel. The place was just a few moments walk from her father-in-law's house and, if she was needed, the company were always very accommodating about time off. Whilst she was her father-in-law's primary carer, her work at the hotel did provide her with the opportunity to meet other people and to give her some respite from the demands and stress of caring for her elderly relative.

Settled at her desk, she began her work on the new bookings. She decided that around nine she would telephone her husband and check that both he and his father were all right. Her husband was now employed only four days a week as his factory was on short-time working. It meant the he could take on more of the caring role than previously and the paid-for weekend carer was no longer required. That had been a cost that had begun to drain their meagre but hard-worked for resources.

Her work almost complete, she grabbed her mobile and slipped into the back room. In her view it wasn't professional to undertake a personal call whilst at her desk.

As she pushed the door too behind her, Wes, the business associate of Richard Laurent Delacroix, breezed through the foyer of the hotel. He glanced at the empty reception desk, nodded to the porter helping a new guest with bags from a taxi and set off up the street towards the centre of town.

Happy that the two mature men in her life were well and needed nothing from her, Sylvie returned to her post just in time to handle the check in details for the newly arrived guest. Glancing at her watch, she realised it would be another hour before she could take her break. She had her book with her and was looking forward to a lemon tea settled by the window in the back room. With twenty minutes alone she felt sure that she could finish the chapter that she had started the night before. Reading was something that she missed greatly now that Archambault Hervé needed so much of her time.

Hotel Belle Vue was one of a chain of twenty-three establishments that were spread through towns of historic interest, such as Saintes, Angers, Rouen and La Rochelle from the northern coast right down to Bordeaux. Each had the same name as they were all located in or close to grounds that were cultivated and landscaped. Not that hotel Belle Vue Verdon, to use its full company name, had much of a view any longer. Most of the extensive grounds at the back had been sold off after the war for housing and the park that sat across the road had suffered an equal level of shortening. All twenty-three hostelries were boutique hotels offering a minimum of four star service along with individuality and absolute discretion in order to attract business people and discerning tourists as their primary client base. When Sylvie opened the company message that had just popped into her inbox, she knew exactly what to do.

The hotel got two or three requests asking for details about a missing person or a person of interest most months. Of course if the request came from the police it was company policy to provide whatever information was required. But this request was from a private investigation firm and, as always, had been sent out from the company headquarters in Rouen to all twenty-three locations. She was about to delete the message when she noticed the picture of the individual. She felt an alarming flutter in her stomach.

"But that's the man we saw two days ago at *papa*'s," she whispered to herself. Her desk phone rang and the display showed that it was the guest in room 8. She picked up the call, handled the query and replaced the handset.

She turned to her computer screen and gazed at the picture of the man in front of her. After a tussle with her conscience Sylvie printed out the company message. Retrieving the printout, she folded it and hastily shoved it in the pocket of her jacket.

"I'll let *papa* decide," she said.

saturday, september 22nd, 10.38

Tomek had a monumental hangover. Despite having showered and shaved at his place in the *Quartiers Nords*, neither his temper nor his headache had improved. And there was that problem he needed to solve, too. As he pulled up in the side street, he changed into reverse and moved the van into the top of *rue des Licornes*. Grabbing a large bunch of keys, he edged between the van and the scaffolding, round to the back of the building. He unlocked the large heavy padlock on the bar across the door in the tiny courtyard and let himself in. Descending to the basement, he shouted for Olivier. There was no response. As he approached the locked door where the Brats were kept he shouted again.

The only response that came was the sound of New Brat beating on the door and shouting to be let out. The noise was echoing through his aching head. He released the padlock and chain. Pulling out the Colt 45, he slid the door open.

"Shut it!" He waved the gun in Pierre's face. The boy backed away. Benoît made a dash for the open door but Tomek was too quick for him. He stretched out his arm, grabbed the boy by the throat and threw him onto the ground. Winded, Benoît scrambled backwards using his elbows and heels.

Tomek advanced on Pierre, the gun at the boy's nose.

"Shut up," he shouted. "More noise," he took two strides forward, "and yer'll be set to run. Don't even know what that means, do yer, Brat?" An evil smile crossed his face. "It's my special kind of hunting, Brat. So... You wanna be set to run?" He advanced, Colt 45 held out in front. "That what you want, eh?"

His victim retreated. Hitting the dusty grey stone of the wall behind, Pierre froze.

"Nothing to say, huh?" He took two more steps until they stood toe to toe. Jabbing the barrel of the gun into the youngster's cheek, he pushed his head to the side and held it there, cold hard metal pressuring through skin, into the wall.

"Now, 'ow many bullets yer think I got in 'ere?"

A pair of eyes squinched shut; a whimper and Pierre's small body trembled.

"'Ow many? Could be one, might be six or... What do yer think?"

Twisting the pistol further into the soft, smooth flesh, he grinned, raised his chin and let out a roar of laughter. Snapping his attention back to his prey's face, he paused as a well-recognised odour reached his nostrils. He breathed it in. Looking down on the warm straw-coloured pool that was still forming between the child's grey-socked feet, he grimaced.

"Gross, man! That's just gross." He stepped back, gun at arm's length and slowly squeezed the trigger.

"No! Don't!" Olivier was in the doorway. Tomek spun around and fired. Olivier fell backwards. A pool of blood began to creep across the floor and form around his head.

"Traitorous bastard," said Tomek after spitting on the body. He looked Pierre in the eye. "No noise." He backed out of the room, slid the door shut and secured it.

saturday, september 22nd, 11.49

In the 7th *arrondissement*, Jacques left Didier parked in a side street behind an apartment block that stood on the *Corniche* and faced out to sea. It was the location that Didier had followed Delacroix to the previous evening. Walking into the courtyard, he saw Delacroix's parked car. As he drew closer to the back entrance to the building he noticed that numbers had been formed by an arrangement of differently coloured stones in one of the empty parking places. He checked the empty space next to Delacroix's car. That read 5. The next empty space, two cars further on, read 9.

"So you're in space 6," he muttered to himself as he reached the back door of the building. Beside the door was a series of buzzers, but each one only had a number. Pressing the buzzers for all the odd numbered apartments he waited until someone answered.

"Delivery for number 4," he said as the owner of number 3 answered their buzzer. The door locking mechanism clicked open and Jacques was in. He walked through to the front. The post boxes were fixed to the wall in two rows of six on the left-hand side of the main entrance. He went straight to the box at the end of the first row. The box for apartment 6 was labelled, 'G BONHEUR'. Just to be sure he hadn't looked at the wrong row he checked the box immediately below it. That had yet another name and, as there were two first names in full it was clear the apartment belonged to a married couple.

Getting his phone out, he quickly took some photos of the wall of post boxes and strode through to the back entrance and out of the door. Using the same ruse again he pressed the buzzer for apartment 12.

When the owner answered he said he had a delivery and gave the name on the post box for apartment 11.

"That's across the hallway, number 11," said the female voice over the intercom.

Jacques left the building. *So why do you need a different name, Richard Laurent Delacroix?*

"Anything?" Asked Didier as Jacques got back into the passenger seat.

"He's parked in the space for apartment 6 but the name on the post box is completely different." Jacques jotted down the details on a page in his notebook, ripped it out and handed it to Didier. "Can we run a check on that please? I'll keep watch."

Didier pulled out his phone and texted Maxim with the details. Just as he completed that task Jacques' phone rang. He checked the display, it was Christophe Renner.

"*Allo*... Yes... OK... And it's the street and not the bar... Yes, please forward it... OK...Thanks." He ended the call. "Monsieur Renner. Tomo has sent another text, *rue des Licornes* at 14.30 this afternoon. Leave Delacroix, we need to plan."

saturday, september 22nd, 14.00

In Verdon-le-Grand, her shift complete, Madame Sylvie Hervé collected her book and her bag and left the hotel. She hurried out of the front entrance, around the corner and into *rue des Déportés Martyrs*, walking briskly down the street, anxious to get to her father-in-law's as soon as possible.

"*Papa*," she shouted a soon as she came through the front door. "It's me." She marched straight into Archambault's front room. But the old man wasn't there. She pulled the net curtain across and looked over to number 38. The car was absent and there was no sign of anyone at the property.

She dashed through the house and out into the garden where her father-in-law sat in one of the garden chairs and her husband was weeding the nearby flowerbeds.

"*Papa!*" They both jolted to attention as she appeared in the garden. "*Papa*, thank goodness you're not asleep."

The old man looked up at her, confusion in his eyes. "Sylvie?"

She pulled a second garden chair closer and sat down. "*Papa*, the man at number 38 with the black car," she pulled the folded printout from her jacket pocket, straightened it and gave it to Archambault. "Is that him?"

The old man put on his spectacles and scrutinised the picture. "Yes, that's him. That's Old Vauquelin."

The use of the name brought Sylvie's husband across the small patch of grass and away from his work.

"Let me see?"

The old man handed the printout over. "I told you he'd be back."

Monsieur Valentin Hervé, Archambault's son, glanced at the photo. He shook his head. "I don't really remember that much about Old Vauquelin, but I do remember the two sons. I was at school at the same time as them," he said to Sylvie. "Old Vauquelin would be about *papa*'s age if he were still alive. And the sons... One was in the same class as me and the other was a couple of years younger. Neither of them looked like this man."

"But we've seen the man in the picture two or three times this week and each time *papa* has been convinced that it is Vauquelin," said Sylvie.

Her husband shook his head. "Dead some years ago and you know that, so why are you indulging *papa* like this? You know we have to try to keep him as much in the present as possible."

Sylvie sighed. "I'm sorry and you're right, I shouldn't have let my curiosity get the better of me." She took the print out back and scrunched it up. "I'll make *papa* some tea."

"And bring me a beer, please, when you come back." Her husband returned to his weeding.

In the kitchen, Sylvie was about to throw the printout away when an idea came to her. She filled the kettle, set it to boil and scurried off into the front room. Opening the doors on the dresser, she rummaged inside until she found what she was looking for. Seated on the edge of her father-in-law's armchair, the old photograph album on her knee, she began to turn the pages. Towards the back she stopped and looked closely at a school photograph. Three rows of students, one for each of the three most senior years at the *lycée,* all looking serious in the sunshine. She smiled as she recognised the much younger and teenage face of the student standing in the back row at the end on the left. It was Valentin, in his last year. She scanned the printed names at the bottom on the mount. Vauquelin, the son in the same year as her husband, was the seventh boy in from the left. Checking the names again she found another Vauquelin and searching the front row on the photograph, she gazed at that face. The evidence before her was irrefutable.

Making her way back to the kitchen, she flicked the

switch on the kettle to bring it back to the boil. Smoothing out the printout, she looked at the face. By the time the kettle had clicked off again she had made her decision.

saturday, september 22nd, 14.23

In Marseille, Jacques had left Didier at the same table in Bar 55 that he had used the previous evening. He knew his colleague would have a clear view of the route that their mark had used to get to the bar for his meeting with Fournier and Delacroix. Jacques was in the car parked in the road leading to the top of *rue des Licornes*. He was waiting for a signal from Didier.

At 14.24, he heard 'mark approaching' in his ear-piece. It was what he'd been waiting for. He reached over to the passenger seat and delved into the glove compartment. In there was an ornamental replica real-sized Colt 45. It belonged to Didier and had been a retirement present from his eldest son. Jacques tucked the gun into his old service gun holster under his jacket.

"Mark ordering," said Didier through the wire.

Jacques thumped the steering wheel. "Damn it!" Hand on the keys in the ignition he wondered whether to start the engine now and let it run.

"Waiter just delivered a beer," came through his ear-piece.

Changing his mind he sat back and tried to relax. *Be patient. Keep calm.* He stared at his fingers drumming on the steering wheel, but was unable to bring them under control. *Come on.* Jacques checked the rear-view mirror and scanned the street for anything untoward. *Come on. Let's do this.* Needing to do something he started the car.

"Am moving car round," he said into his mic. He shifted into first and pulled the car round the corner. He nosed it up to the top entrance of *rue des Licornes*. A rusty white Peugeot delivery van was there, its nose pointing out ready for a quick getaway if needed. *Didier's snout mentioned a small white van.* He jotted the registration number down in his notebook. Leaving the keys in the ignition, Jacques got out and gently pushed the door closed. Moving to the far side of the van, he edged between the vehicle and the wall of the building and ducked down.

"In place," he whispered into the mic. Carefully he removed the replica gun from his holster and edged a little further along the street. He could see the nose of the van but very little of the rest of the road because of the curvature. He strained to listen. There were no voices. He'd expected to hear voices. *Must be handling today's trade alone.* Jacques didn't like the look or feel of that thought. He tried to banish it from his mind.

"Mark on the move," came though his earpiece.

Jacques braced himself. *Can't get this wrong.*

"Blonde woman following," came from Didier.

Jacques waited. He couldn't see their mark but now he could hear him.

"Let's party together sometime," the man said. The clatter of the woman's heels on the cobbles meant the transaction was done.

That's supply. Chargeable. Jacques was satisfied that an arrest could be made. A chargeable offence had to be witnessed and Tomek had just given him one. He edged a little closer. He heard footsteps and froze.

"Man in jeans in street. Am following," came through the wire.

Jacques stayed down. He heard their mark greet his customer and then the man was moving away again. *Supply, second count. Chargeable.*

"Approaching," and Jacques was on the move. Silently, he came up behind their mark.

"New customer, who sent—"

The replica gun jabbed in the centre of the back of his head, their mark froze. "Do exactly as I say. Hands above you head."

The dealer complied.

"On your knees," said Jacques. The man dropped down to the ground.

Didier frisked him and located his weapon, a Colt 45.

"Arms outstretched and lie flat on the ground."

There was a moment's hesitation. Didier put the real gun to the side of the man's head. "Flat on the ground," he repeated.

In the next second the dealer was prostrate. Grabbing his right arm at the same time as Jacques grabbed the left, they forced both arms up his back.

"If this is about Bonner's money. Tell 'im I'm getting it sorted."

Jacques cast Didier a confused glance. Recognising the name, he decided to play along anyway.

"It's Monsieur Bonheur to you," he said, making the correct pronunciation clear.

"OK. Monsieur Bonheur. He'll get 'is money. I just need a couple of days."

"Thanks for letting me know but I don't take messages. Now, where are your runners?"

"What!"

Didier made a great play of checking the ammunition chamber of the real revolver. "One round fired. You've got five more opportunities to tell us where your runners are."

Jacques tightened his grip and pulled his victim's left arm further up his back. The man squirmed and let out a low squeal of pain.

"Basement," he spluttered.

"Get his phone and check all his pockets."

Didier handed Jacques the real gun and continued his search. He dropped a bunch of keys, a wallet, some house keys and vehicle keys on the ground. In one of the lower pockets of the cargo pants the man was wearing, he found a knife. He moved everything out of reach.

"OK. Call it in."

Jacques held their captive whilst his colleague formalised the arrest they had just made. As soon as Didier was able to take over, Jacques passed him the real gun. Grabbing the bunches of keys, he disappeared behind the sheeting and to the backdoor. The bar had been removed and laid on the ground. Jacques went in. He checked his surroundings. In the distance, he heard the sirens of the police vehicles approaching. He moved stealthily through the empty building. Finding the stairs to the basement he started down. As he progressed he became aware of a familiar metallic odour. The realisation that he could be too late hit him like a thunderbolt. He stopped for a moment and swallowed back his fear.

The sirens in the street above were much closer. Jacques took a deep breath and moved on. At the bottom of the steps he looked left and right. The smell was stronger from the right. He moved slowly forward and caught sight of a sliding door secured with chain and a padlock ahead on his left. Another four steps closer and on his right he saw the remains of Tomek's work.

His handkerchief around his mouth and nose, Jacques approached. His former police training taking over, he made a quick check of the body. "No visible sign of life," he said as though he were addressing a colleague. The round dark red mark in the centre of the forehead, the pool of blood that surrounded the body were proof enough. But he still had to check for signs of life. Placing his fingers on the right wrist he waited. *No pulse.*

"Body in basement to right of stairs," he said into his mic. "From the look of him I would say the body fits the description of Olivier Duchamp."

"Got that," replied Didier.

Turning his attention to the sliding door, he fiddled with the various keys until he found the one that fitted the padlock. Unsure of what he might find, he gently slid the door open. He remained on the threshold. The room appeared to be empty. He looked up at the narrow windows at the top of the wall opposite. The blue flashing lights of the police cars were casting eerie shadows on the floor and across the walls. Over by one wall stood three washing machines. *Behind those is the only place in here to hide, if anyone is here.*

"Pierre?" He thought he heard something on his right. "Pierre, it's Jacques."

From behind a large washing machine, a grubby face with a black eye peeped out. A second later, and Pierre was on his feet and running across the floor. He flung his arms around Jacques and let out a wail.

"Tomek shot the other one," he blurted out and a gush of tears followed almost immediately.

Jacques put the replica gun back in his holster. "It's alright. You're safe now." As he looked up, he saw another face appear from behind the washing machine.

"It's OK," he said beckoning to the second boy. "The police are here." The boy hesitated, moved a step or two closer and then stopped. Jacques extricated himself from Pierre's arms. Bending down, he put his hand on the boy's shoulder.

"I need you both to be brave and to be calm," he said looking from one child to the other. "You will need to go with the police. They will take you to the station and they will make sure that you are seen by a doctor, OK?"

Pierre glanced at his friend, who edged forward, and they both nodded.

Standing straight, Jacques spoke into his mic. "Two boys here, Didier. Pierre is one of them. I need an officer down here right now."

Almost on cue two members from the city police appeared in the doorway.

"Jacques Forêt," he said. "These children are witnesses. They need your protection, medical attention and to be interviewed." He ushered the boys forward. Once they were in custody, he pulled out his phone and removed his earpiece, then dialled.

"Martin, it's Jacques. Pierre is safe…"

saturday, september 22nd, 19.28

Inspecteur Graves of the city police was the embodiment of everything his name conveyed. His hair was greying, his complexion was equally grey and the life-long engrained expression on his face serious and sombre. It was clear to Jacques, from the grilling he'd been given, that *Inspecteur* Graves ran his team with an iron fist, that he had a keen eye for detail, and that he would not rest until every possible angle had been covered. Despite that, Jacques had managed not to mention Christophe Renner. He had admitted to working with Fournier. It was a fact that was too easily traceable for him to do otherwise. But for Delacroix, he had managed to keep that identity to himself. However, the *Inspecteur*'s gratitude was fulsome as he shook hands with Jacques and Didier.

"Thank you for all your help, Monsieur Forêt," said Graves. "Tomek Železný, the only one of his many names that is real, is a criminal I've been wanting to put behind bars for more than two years."

Leaving the gloom of the central police station Jacques and Didier made their way towards the harbour. Out in the fresh, light breeze around the *Vieux Port*, Didier rolled his shoulders back. "I'm hungry," he said.

Jacques grinned. "Me too. We'll find somewhere to eat and then drive back first thing tomorrow morning."

As they strolled along the quay, Didier couldn't stop himself from taking a closer look at the yacht that they watched berth the previous afternoon.

"That looks as though it was built in the 1920s," he said. "There's around €200 to €300,000, just sitting there, Jacques." As Didier turned to face him, the light in his eyes was bright and vibrant. "Add on mooring fees, maintenance costs and well…"

"The words are telling me one thing, Didier, but your face is telling me quite a different story."

Didier laughed out loud. "I feel like some *moules* tonight," he said as he turned and strolled along the port to the same restaurant they'd used the day before.

The place was beginning to fill with evening diners. Jacques and Didier took a table in an out-of-the-way corner. The two men barely glanced at the menu and when the waiter arrived to take their order, Didier ordered for them both.

"A bottle of *sauvignon blanc* and *moules marinières* for us both, please."

The waiter disappeared and returned immediately with a basket containing a generous portion of *pain* that had been sliced. When he brought the wine, Didier tasted it and then waved him away. Jacques poured them each a glass and they settled back in their chairs.

"I hope they throw the book at Tomek," said Didier.

"Agreed," said Jacques. "But this is Marseille and the Devereux brothers have some very powerful allies." Jacques savoured his wine. "And if Fournier is involved, then… Who knows?"

"You think he might be bent?"

"I don't know. But I do have an unresolved question. Three years ago a traveller went missing, Alain Lavoie. When we eventually found his body, he'd been poisoned. We also found a phone which had one name in the contacts list. Fournier's."

"An old snout," suggested Didier.

"At the time, that was my conclusion and I had no evidence for any other scenario, but I was never sure. Now, I can see other possibilities, but I still have no hard evidence." Jacques took a drink of his wine.

"So, Lavoie could have been an informant or a carrier. Is that what you're thinking?"

Jacques shook his head. "Either is possible. But it's up to

Graves, now. If there is a connection to Lavoie through Fournier, he's the man to find it."

"It'll be interesting to find out what the ballistic reports say about the cache of arms that Graves' men found in the van."

"He's not obliged to tell us anything, Didier." Jacques took another sip of his wine.

"At least we've got something on Delacroix." Didier reached for the basket and offered it to Jacques, and then took a piece of the *pain* for himself.

"Have we?" Jacques put his forefinger and thumb on the base of the stem of his glass and twisted it through a quarter turn. "What have we really got on Delacroix?" The glass moved through another turn.

Didier glanced across the restaurant and sighed. "You're right. That meeting yesterday evening…"

"It could have been anything." Jacques' glass continued through another revolution.

"But associating with a known criminal—"

The waiter interrupted Didier and placed two bowls of mussels on the table along with a side order of *frites*. He returned a few moments later with a small finger bowl for each of them. The aroma of the sea, the parsley, the garlic was too much and they both attacked the shellfish.

Half way through his bowl, his initial hunger sated, Jacques paused and dunked his fingers in the small bowl of water and wiped his hands on his serviette.

"Going back to Delacroix," he said taking another piece of the *pain* from the basket. "To be seen associating with a known criminal isn't a crime in itself. But it does raise questions. A known drug dealer, a senior *gendarme* and a supposedly legitimate business man."

Jacques looked beyond his colleague as he let his mind search through all the plausible possibilities, his hands automatically tearing chunks from the *pain*.

"The most damning connection," said Jacques, his attention returning to his meal and his companion, "is the money. Tomek mentioned money owed to Monsieur

Bonheur." He dropped a chunk of bread into his bowl of mussels, and once it was saturated with the buttery juices, he fished it out again with the empty shell he held in his hand.

"Which would suggest that Delacroix is the supplier and Fournier is being paid off to keep quiet and inform on any possible police interest."

Jacques grinned. "And Graves is just the man to follow the money."

Didier stared. "Are we abandoning our current work on the Delacroix?"

"Not entirely, no. I'm still not convinced that he is who he says he is. Here in Marseille, he's known, and referred to, as Monsieur Bonheur…" Jacques shrugged.

"And in my experience," said Didier, "when a man needs more than one name, it's often for fraudulent purposes."

Jacques nodded. "We'll leave first thing tomorrow," he said as he popped another mussel into his mouth and discarded the shell on the rim of the plate the bowl was on. "I want to get back to Mende as early as possible."

Didier nodded and ripped a chunk from a piece of bread on his side plate and dipped it in the juices at the bottom of his bowl.

"I'd like to go straight to the office when we get back. I want to spend a couple of hours catching up with Maxim and I want to make sure that the *police municipale* in Mende have found the third boy and then…" He downed the last mouthful of wine in his glass. "And then I want to get home to Beth and Lucien."

"When we've finished eating, I'll call Maxim and set that up," said Didier as he refilled their glasses.

sunday, september 23rd, 10.06

Maxim had arrived at the office that morning with a supply of *croissants* and *pains au chocolat*. Tucking into their pastries in Jacques' office, Maxim and Didier had gathered at Jacques' desk with a constant supply of coffee.

"Let's start with Olivier Duchamp," said Jacques. "Whatever work you were following up on Duchamp, you can shelve, Maxim. Regrettably, he didn't make it. The city police in Marseille will be handling everything in connection with his murder."

"I hadn't been able to find much, anyway," said Maxim. "The work on the Delacroix case has kind of taken over my desk since you left on Friday." He helped himself to a *croissant*.

"What about Monsieur Buhot? I had some doubts about him before we left," said Didier.

"I think we can discount him," replied Maxim. He presented both Jacques and Didier with copies of some newspaper articles. "Monsieur Buhot was a teacher at a *lycée* in St-Étienne until thirty years ago. A female student accused him of sexual harassment. The case made the papers. But it's the interview on the last page that is the most interesting. It appeared in a local magazine in St-Étienne about eighteen months after the original accusation and immediately after the girl had finally admitted that she had falsely accused Monsieur Buhot."

Didier flicked straight to the last page and began reading. "I knew there was something…" He underlined a sentence. "Listen to this, Jacques. 'Because of that girl, I've lost a job I loved, my family, and for what?'" Didier looked up. "That explains what he meant when he said his family was distant."

"If he's experienced that kind of investigation, it would also explain his reticence to speak to anyone asking questions."

"I think we can close that line of enquiry," said Didier, handing the papers back to Maxim.

"What about the third boy? Has he been found?"

"I rang the *police municipale* as soon as I came in this morning. Daniel St-Jean was discovered yesterday in an old warehouse at 17.19 along with the two mopeds we, and the local police, have been looking for. He was first reported missing by his father in St-Étienne three months ago. Two days later, when the police went to see his father, they discovered that Monsieur St-Jean had left that address. They are still looking for Monsieur St-Jean."

Jacques nodded. "At least we have been able to help them with one missing person case. How was the boy?"

"Tired, hungry but otherwise in reasonably good shape."

"Good. Delacroix next." Jacques got up and went across to his large whiteboard. Pulling the magnetic strips away that divided the written notes into columns and rows, he discarded them on the floor. Taking the rubber, he swept it across the board.

Maxim stood. "But I…"

Jacques turned and saw the scowl on his colleagues face. "Apologies, Maxim. I should have said that I read your detailed updates as soon as I got here, whilst you were getting all your papers together."

Maxim smiled and resumed his seat.

Jacques crossed back to his desk and collected his coffee. He pulled the small table from in front of the three easy chairs on one side of the room across to where he stood. With a marker in his hand, he reached up to the board and wrote as he spoke.

"*Fermier* Guy Delacroix died from a fatal heart attack following an accident." He noted the board with the abbreviations and added the date in his clear round script.

"I would like us to start with Guy Delacroix," he said.

"What certain facts do we know about him?" He looked across at Maxim who leafed through the large file in which everything in connection with Richard Laurent Delacroix was stored.

Locating the details he needed, he read, "Born in 1933, the second son of Bernard Delacroix."

Jacques added the details to the board. "And the eldest son?"

"Francis, born 1931."

Jacques added that to the board and included lines showing the family relationship between the three names. "What about the next generation, Maxim?"

"The older brother, Francis first. He married Marie in 1955 and his first son, Richard Laurent Delacroix, was born in 1966. He and his family emigrated to Canada in 1968 where their second son, Jérôme, was born that same year."

The family tree partially complete Jacques moved to the other side of the board and added the additional details before prompting Maxim for the details for Guy Delacroix.

"*Fermier* Guy Delacroix married Clémence Vauquelin in 1956. In 1957, they had a daughter, Émilie, who died when she was two days old. Clémence died a few days after that."

Jacques sipped his coffee as he stepped back from the white board and considered the information recorded. "So, we know that Richard Laurent Delacroix inherited the farm from his uncle, so there must have been a will or some form of inheritance planning, otherwise the farm would have been split to accommodate *la réserve*." Jacques turned to Maxim for an answer.

"That's where this gets complicated, Jacques. There are no formal wills. I've checked and double checked."

Jacques frowned at the information on the board. "At what generation of the family are there no formal wills?"

"From the top. Bernard Delacroix downwards."

"So automatic inheritance rights would apply," said Didier. "And depending on the order of the relevant deaths, Richard Laurent Delacroix may have had no right to the whole of the farm in the first place."

"We need those details, Maxim."

"OK, I think I've got most of it on my desk, but I'll check and get any extra data." He looked up at the board and Jacques noticed the same questioning expression on his face when he was unsure of whether he should say something or not.

"What is it, Maxim?"

"Just some odd coincidences. I'm sure that's all it is." Maxim flicked through the Delacroix file and picked out a sheaf of papers that contained copies of newspaper reports. "On those sheets are copies of articles relating to Jérôme Delacroix, the second son of the brother of who went to Canada. He was reported missing at the age of ten. The case was never resolved because a body was never found, nor was the child. But he wasn't legally declared dead until 1998."

"And who sought the action for the legal declaration?"

"His older brother, Richard Laurent Delacroix."

"That's interesting," said Jacques. "Such an action requires a formal application to the courts and evidence to be supplied along with any searches that the court may request before deciding the action."

"Isn't that usually requested about seven years after the disappearance?"

"Yes, it is, Maxim. So why wait so long? Unless—"

"There's money or assets involved," interrupted Didier.

"Yes, a will, an insurance policy, land or property."

"I'll check that out," said Maxim.

"Something else," added Didier. "If Jérôme's body was never found and the police case was never resolved, there is the remote possibility that he could actually still be alive but using a different name and a new personal history."

Jacques gazed at the whiteboard. "I think it's unlikely, but it is possible." He turned to Maxim. "Those court papers will be a matter of public record, Maxim. Can you get copies please."

Maxim made a note.

Jacques returned to his desk and sat down. His

handiwork displayed before him he let his eyes move over the details.

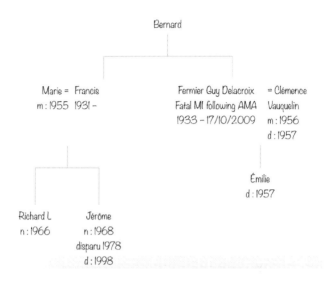

"Maxim, we need to fill in some of these gaps. Bernard Delacroix, we know he didn't leave a will, but when did he die? Second, his son Francis, when did he die and when did his wife die? If there are no wills at all in this family, then knowing when these individuals died will help us to understand what, if anything, Richard Laurent Delacroix really is entitled to."

Maxim nodded. "I'll get onto it."

Jacques glanced at his watch. "I really need to get home to Beth," he said. "Maxim, you were also going to ask for information about Delacroix from a number of other sources. Did we get anything useful in response?"

Maxim reached across for the file and pulled out a typed report. Jacques glanced through it. At the end was a useful table and he went to the white board and added the extra information below the Delacroix family tree.

"This Madame Sylvie Hervé, she is absolutely positive that it was Richard Laurent Delacroix she saw."

"Yes, she is certain. At first she said his name was Monsieur Vauquelin, but when I pressed her about that she became unsure. What she was very certain about was the house that Richard Laurent Delacroix was using definitely belonged to the Vauquelin family, that it had not been sold and that the two brothers have never agreed on how to deal with the property. She also said that if he was using the name Vauquelin, that he couldn't be one of the sons, because she has an old school photo and neither of the two sons has ever had black hair. One was blond and the other was red-haired."

"Again, we need to check for a will," said Jacques. "And ask Madame if we can see the photograph."

"Already done that, Jacques, and she will email a copy to us as soon as she can." He paused briefly, checking his notes. "The address in Marseille you asked me to check. That apartment was purchased by an American company called WRD Associates five years ago. A Monsieur Guillaume Bonheur rents it but is rarely ever there. According to the *Concierge* for the building Monsieur Bonheur has business overseas all the time and is only resident for a few weeks each year."

"What about the company directors for WRD Associates," asked Didier.

"I'm checking into that, but I have nothing yet."

"Anything from any of the other locations on my list?"

"Only from Saintes. Two different hotels recognised Delacroix but both gave a different name. In one he was registered as Christian Salle and in the other he was registered as François Morisot."

"And both places are certain of the name and that it is Delacroix?"

Maxim nodded.

Jacques looked at his watch. "I need to get home," he said. "Why someone would need so many different identities is puzzling...unless?"

"Fraud," said Didier. "In my experience it is always about some form of fraud."

"Hmm. Madame Sylvie Hervé, Maxim. Get back onto her and question her closely about the Vauquelin family. Find out everything you can." Jacques stood and shook his head. "I don't know where we are going with this. But something isn't right."

sunday, september 23rd, 13.08

The blue waters of the lake between Messandrierre and Rieutort were shimmering in the afternoon sunshine. In the shade of the trees, Jacques – courtesy of his sister Thérèse – had spread out the picnic that she had prepared for them. His sister's words had echoed through his mind more than once. 'You need some time to yourselves,' she'd said. *And Beth has had precious little of that since Lucien was born.* 'You need to make that time' was the other phrase of his sister's that kept revolving around his head. He watched as Beth helped herself to a piece of quiche. She'd barely touched the *charcuterie*, but the quiche and salad seemed to be finding favour. He studied her face. There was a little more colour in her cheeks and she didn't seem to look quite as exhausted as she had done earlier in the week.

"What?" she asked.

Jacques snapped out of his reverie. "I was just thinking how much better you look. There's some colour in your cheeks." He picked at his piece of bread.

"I'm feeling a little better today." Her phone pinged and she picked it up instantly. Another idea of his sister's. "Oh look," said Beth, turning the phone to face him. "Lucien in his carrycot."

Jacques wondered how long it had taken Thérèse to persuade Beth that half-hourly texts containing a picture would be all she would need to know that Lucien was safe and happy.

"We should make a point of doing something like this as often as we can," said Jacques.

Beth's faced clouded and there was a tremor in her voice when she spoke. "But what about Lucien?"

"Lucien will be with us," said Jacques taking hold of her hand. "I just meant that it will be good for us both to do something away from my work, the apartment, the city and everything that means stress for us both. Do something as the new family that we are now."

Beth smiled. It was the first time in over three months that he'd seen the glimmer of the light in her eyes that had previously always been there for him alone.

"I think I like that idea," she said. She toyed with the salad leaves on her plate. "Maybe we could start coming to the chalet again at weekends."

Jacques poured a drop of wine into her glass. "I would like that, too," he said. "We will need to make some changes though. It's not a very child-friendly place at the moment."

"Hmm. I can't really remember what it's like. I've been... I seem to have... I feel like I've been in some sort of nebulous fog for months."

He decided not to comment. He refilled his own glass and reached into the hamper for some cheese.

"We have some Brie, some Camembert, your favourite, and some *Pélardon*, my favourite. What would you like?"

"Nothing at the moment. Maybe later."

Jacques removed the film covering the plate of cheese and cut himself a chunk of the *Pélardon*. He broke off a piece of bread from the *pain* and added it to his plate.

"The sun on the water is fabulous this afternoon. I wish I'd brought my camera." It was the first time in months that she had mentioned or even hinted at the hobby that had become her work since moving to France.

"Perhaps I can help with that," he said as he stood, picked up the car keys and disappeared out of the clearing. A couple of moments later, he was back with her camera bag which he placed on the bench beside her. Beth's reaction wasn't quite what he had hoped for. She stared at the bag, almost as though it were accusing her of some heinous crime of neglect. *Ahh, too much too soon, again.*

"My camera bag," she reached out and ran her hand

across the top. "I can't remember when I last used this."

"About six months ago," he said. "The morning sickness had been quite severe and you'd become almost afraid to leave the apartment."

Beth frowned and looked away as though trying to recall what he'd described. He saw her shake her thoughts from her mind. Pulling the bag towards her, she unzipped it and stared at the contents. "I don't know if I can do this anymore."

"I think you can."

He watched as she retrieved her camera. Once it was in her hands, instinct guided her every move. Intuition led her through the necessary checks and helped her decide on the settings. Standing, she moved away from the table towards the edge of the lake. For a few moments Jacques watched her at work. Looking up to gauge the angle of the sun. Moving into the shadow and adjusting the lens. And then she stopped and glanced back at him. There were tears in her eyes, a look of horror on her face. He jumped up immediately and dashed across to her.

"I haven't got a single photo of Lucien," she wailed. "How could I have been so thoughtless?"

Jacques put his arms around her. "You haven't been yourself," he said. "Your pregnancy wasn't easy and the labour was long and difficult. You've had a very difficult six, seven months or so."

She wiped her hand across her face. Jacques fished out his handkerchief and gave it to her. He led her back to the picnic table.

"There will be plenty of opportunities to take pictures of Lucien as he grows. But, if you want, we can go home now and get a photo straight away. Of Lucien, of the three of us and with my sister too if you wish."

Beth nodded. "I owe Thérèse a lot." Her phone pinged again. As she read the text her smile returned. She put her camera away and slung the bag over her shoulder as she always used to. Strolling back to the car she slipped her hand into his, entwining her slim fingers through his. It was the first real sign of affection that he'd seen in a long time. *You're back.*

***

In the apartment in Marseille that was owned by WRD Associates and rented to a Monsieur Bonheur, Richard Laurent Delacroix was packing hurriedly. The telephone conversation he'd just had with Gilles Fournier had caused him great concern. To know that Jacques Forêt was the reason for the interruption to his drugs supply line was galling.

From the safe in the back of the built-in wardrobes in the master bedroom he removed every scrap of evidence that he had been there. Money. Bank cards. Passports in numerous names. Wills, property deeds and a data stick. Everything went into his briefcase.

Moving through the apartment like a whirlwind he took only his own personal items from the bathroom, living space and kitchen area. Everything else had to be left so that the property could be returned to its original purpose, available for rent in order to generate legitimate income.

Lastly he telephoned the cleaning company he used and arranged for them to come in the next day and deep clean the whole apartment. In the foyer of the block he removed the nametag 'G BONHEUR' from the post box and slotted it into the back pocket of his jeans. That would meet its end in the wood burning stove in the farmhouse in Messandrierre. With everything in the back of the car he got behind the wheel.

"Where next?" He turned the keys in the ignition, reversed out of the designated parking spot and was gone.

monday, september 24th, 09.37

At the central station in Mende, Jacques, Beth and Lucien said their goodbyes to Thérèse.

Jacques handed the car keys to Beth and left her and Lucien to wait with his sister for the train that she was taking back to Paris. As he strode across the city to his office, he wondered if he'd made the right decision. Beth had stopped driving early in the pregnancy, and although she seemed more her old self at breakfast, he still could not shake the nagging doubt that he should have stayed with her. Driven her to the photographic studio and shop himself. But she'd insisted on getting back behind the wheel. *I suppose I should be grateful that Thérèse chose the 9.50 instead of the earlier train.* The thought provided little consolation, but it did mean that Beth would have missed the worst of the rush-hour traffic as she drove to her studio.

Crossing the *boulevard* to the Vaux building, he breezed in and took the stairs to the fourth floor.

"*Bonjour.*" He stepped into the general office. "I'm meeting Alain Vaux in three minutes," he said, checking his watch. "As soon as I'm done we'll pick up from where we left off yesterday."

In his own office, he switched on the coffee machine, placed his mobile next to his desk phone and logged into the IT network. A light tap on his door and Alain Vaux, Chairman of the Board of Directors, walked in.

"I understand congratulations are in order," he said as he crossed the room and sat opposite Jacques. "You found young Pierre safe and well and effected the rescue of two other boys as well. Impressive, Jacques." Alain was often short on praise, but, being the hardheaded businessman that he was, he could be relied upon to use factual statements as a means to convey his thoughts.

"Thank you, but that's not why you're here, Alain, is it?"

Alain sat back and crossed one leg over the other. "No. You've got what you want, Jacques. The Board have voted in favour of the buy-out. The contract is with the legal team for some minor adjustments to wording. It will be with you later today. If you could go through it carefully and let me have a signature, we can move forward as quickly as you like."

Jacques took a moment to process the words. He'd expected more delay, prevarication even. "That's... That's great news, Alain. Thank you." He stood and held out his hand. Alain reciprocated.

"There is just one thing." Alain straightened his tie. "A request really. And it's a vanity, I know. But, somewhere on your marketing material for your new independent company would you consider including some form of wording that will detail who founded the original business."

A vanity indeed. Jacques grinned. "Of course, Alain, and I hope that we will be able to work together amicably in the future as well."

Alain nodded and took his leave. As the office door closed, Jacques allowed a small snigger to escape. *A small price for a vanity.* His mobile rang.

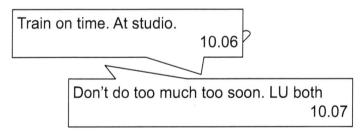

Jacques strode over to the windows and looked down on the street below. Hands in his trouser pockets he watched the people, but only seemed to see the mothers with children in prams or pushchairs. *What will the future hold*

for all of you? He smiled to himself. He knew he should tell his team the good news. *It won't hurt to keep it to myself just for a little while longer.* The sound of a siren from the street as an emergency services vehicle raced to an incident drew his attention back to the business of the day. Looking down, he saw a familiar figure crossing the road.

"So, you're back from Marseille." He turned to return to his desk. Retrieving his mobile he dialled the restaurant in Messandrierre.

"Gaston, I've just seen Richard Laurent Delacroix here in Mende, I expect he will be coming through to the village. If he comes into the restaurant today can you let me know, please?... No, nothing special, just keeping tabs on him at the moment, that's all... OK. Thanks."

Unable to keep the news about the buy-out to himself any longer, he walked through to the general office.

"The Board have agreed to our terms," he said as he strolled over to Didier's desk.

"Are we officially Jacques Forêt Associates?"

A wide grin on his face Jacques nodded. "Unofficially, yes. The contract will be with me shortly and I need to go through it first and then sign it. I also want to talk to Madame Rouselle. Her husband's family have been farming in Messandrierre for generations. If there's a hint of anything suspicious, Madame will know. We'll pick up the progress on Delacroix after lunch."

monday, september 24th, 11.49

His business in Mende complete Delacroix let himself into the farmhouse in Messandrierre and locked the door behind him. He ran down the stairs to his office space and slid his briefcase onto the desk, then strode through to his safe, collected the contents and dropped everything onto the nearby table. The bank cards in the name of Guillaume Bonheur he cut in half. The cash he had withdrawn that morning before closing the accounts in the name of Bonheur he placed in a money wallet along with the cash he had brought from the safe in Marseille. Guillaume Bonheur, he had decided, was no longer needed and had to disappear.

Checking through the passports, he lifted out a Canadian, an American and a French one, each in the name of Bonheur. He set those aside with the destroyed cards. The fake rental agreement in the name of Bonheur which he'd created for his use of the WRD apartment in Marseille he tore in half and added it to the pile. He sifted through everything else to assure himself that he had located all items in the name of Bonheur. At the back of his mind there was a nagging thought that he had missed something. Scooping up the various items to be destroyed, he went to the *cave* and into the small room containing the wood burner. Adding logs and the debris, he set it alight.

In his office space he began to repack his briefcase. Seeing the phone he used only when using the identity of Bonheur he quickly prised open the back and removed the sim and threw that into the fire.

Returning to his desk, he switched on the computers. He would need to remove everything and then destroy the hard drives. He plugged in his portable drive and set the machine to run the back up. It would take over two hours.

"And that's just enough time for one last meal." He collected his jacket and took the stairs two at a time.

monday, september 24th, 13.17

Having driven Beth and Lucien back to the apartment, Jacques had returned to work on his motorbike.

"Sorry I'm a bit late," he said as he joined the others in his office.

"*Inspecteur* Graves wants you to call him," said Didier as he placed a note with a phone number on Jacques desk.

"OK, thanks. I'll call him later. What have we got?" He looked at the whiteboard, expecting to see more information, his expectation reduced to disappointment.

"I've been looking at the old man, Bernard Delacroix," said Didier. He glanced down at his notes. "Born in 1898 and died in 1969. He was an only child and took over the farm from his father."

Seeing the marker on his desk, Jacques got up and added the new information to the board. "And was there a will?"

"No, and at the time of the death, Bernard was the only surviving relative with any form of claim to the land. I've also spoken to the *Mairie* in Messandrierre to get some details from the *matrice cadastrale*. The shift of ownership of title of the land confirms what we know already. The land moved from Bernard to Guy to Richard Laurent Delacroix. *Maire* Mancelle gave his permission for us to be supplied with any details we needed immediately. He was also asking when you would next be in the village, Jacques. I think he wants to tell you himself how grateful he is for the safe return of his grandson."

Jacques shrugged. "I think we may be back in the village this weekend. I'll call on him."

"There appears to be nothing of any concern until you look into the circumstances surrounding the death of

Bernard. There was a delay in formalising the death and issuing the certificate," said Didier.

"Yes, and according to Madame Rouselle, her mother-in-law always maintained that the farm was to go the oldest son, Francis. Apparently the two boys always quarrelled and when Guy married a Vauquelin, as far as Bernard Delacroix and his son Francis were concerned, Guy had brought disgrace on the family. Madame Rouselle doesn't know the details of the argument between Bernard Delacroix and the Vauquelin family. She suggested that it was most probably land. The eldest son, Francis, left and then moved to Canada. Madame Rouselle also said that Bernard had let it be widely known that Guy would never get the farm."

"That's interesting, but without a will stating that, we can't be sure. However, it puts a different perspective on Bernard's death. He fell in the barn and suffered a fatal head injury."

Jacques nodded. "Did he really fall or was he pushed?"

"Exactly. I've done some digging, but the death was ruled accidental."

"Something else that Madame Rouselle said was about the funeral for Bernard. Only Guy attended. There were no other family members and the rumour in the village, according to her mother-in-law, was that Guy had never informed his brother that their father was dead."

"What about a will? Did Guy Delacroix ever make a will?"

Didier shook his head. "I've checked and there was no formal will. But there was a letter from Guy stating that it had always been his intention to leave the farm and the property in Messandrierre to his brother's children."

"If that letter is genuine, then presumably that was how Richard Laurent Delacroix could make a claim."

"There are some other pieces of information that have now come to light," said Maxim. "I've been checking the Canadian half of the family and Francis died in 1999, three and half months after his youngest son was formally declared dead. Francis was found dead at the bottom of the stairs."

"But the death was ruled accidental?"

Maxim nodded. "Madame Sylvie Hervé has also been in touch again and we now have the school photograph she mentioned." Maxim placed a printed copy on Jacques desk. "The boy marked out in the back row and the one in the front row are the Vauquelin brothers."

"And she's right. Neither one of those boys could be Delacroix."

Jacques looked at the whiteboard and checked over the information.

"This is all circumstantial, Didier. There's no case here, but we can unsettle him with what we've found and I think we should. Do you still have that photo of Delacroix, Fournier and Tomek at the table in Bar 55 in Marseille?"

Didier checked his phone. "Yes, I'll forward it to you. Do we know where Delacroix is?"

Jacques grinned. "Yes, we do. He's in Messandrierre, and he must still be at the restaurant as Gaston was to alert me when he left."

Jacques' phone beeped. A quick glance and he knew it was the photo from Didier.

"Maxim, give *Inspecteur* Graves Delacroix's name and location and tell him the he is involved with the drugs running. Ask him to get the necessary papers for our police to act on his behalf and tell him that we believe Delacroix is likely to abscond. Didier, you're with me."

The last thing Jacques did was to capture all the information on the whiteboard on his phone.

monday, september 24th, 14.07

In the restaurant in Messandrierre, the last few diners were still at their tables. Gaston was behind the bar, preparing some coffees. Jacques looked around and saw Delacroix at a table by the window, reading the newspaper. He looked in no hurry to leave.

Jacques left Didier at the bar and sauntered across to Delacroix's table. Approaching the table from behind, Jacques noticed a small oblong of card on the floor at the base of one of the back legs of the chair. As he got closer he saw the name 'G BONHEUR' printed on it. He recognised it from the post box in the apartment block. *You must have cleaned out the place in Marseille.*

"Monsieur Delacroix, may I join you?"

Delacroix looked over his paper. "If you want, Forêt, but as soon as Gaston takes my bill and brings me my change, I'll be leaving."

Jacques looked at the small plate containing the bill and some cash. Delacroix's wallet was on the table beside the dish.

"How was Marseille at the weekend?"

"I wouldn't know; I wasn't there." He flexed the pages of his newspaper straight and continued to stare at it.

"Ah, I see. So are you denying that you met Gilles Fournier at a bar in the city this weekend?"

Delacroix shot Jacques a glance. "I don't know what you're talking about, Forêt." He looked across the room to Gaston who was in conversation with Didier. "Gaston," he shouted. "My change if you don't mind."

Jacques pulled out his phone and called up the photo. "That is you, Monsieur Delacroix, isn't it?" He showed the photograph to his interviewee. "And that man there beside you is Gilles Fournier. Would you like to tell me what you were discussing?"

Delacroix roughly folded the newspaper and flung it down on the table. "When, where and with whom I do business is none of your concern." He stood just as two members of the *police municipale* arrived.

"I think you'll find that you are a person of interest in connection with a case that the city police in Marseille are investigating." Jacques stood aside and let his ex-colleagues do their job.

"One last thing," he said, bending down to point out the small piece of card on the floor by Delacroix's chair. "I think this may have been removed from the post box of an apartment block in Marseille. If I'm right it will have your fingerprints on it, Delacroix, or is it Monsieur Bonheur? Perhaps it's really Christian Salle or Monsieur Morisot?"

Jacques watched as the piece of evidence was retrieved and placed in an evidence bag. When he glanced at Delacroix, he saw a murderous look in his eyes as he strained against the hold of the officers.

wednesday, september 26th, 11.34

In his office in Mende, Jacques had allowed Maxim to clean off the whiteboard and replace the information about Delacroix with details of their current cases. The magnetic strips were back in place and the rows and columns all neatly re-arranged. The contract for the buy-out was signed

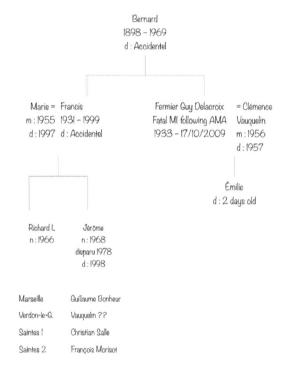

and would be effective from the first of the next month

when Amélie, Maxim's wife, would be returning to work part-time. Her initial task was to manage the publicity around the new identity of the company.

Putting the receiver back on its cradle following his pre-arranged phone call with *Inspecteur* Graves of the city police in Marseille, Jacques let a broad smile move across his face.

"We've got him," he said as he walked through to the general office.

"Good news?" Didier stood and Maxim shoved his computer keyboard away.

"The ballistic reports on the cache of arms found in the drug pusher's van are all back. There are matches for all the boys bodies that we were interested in. There was also a twelve bore shotgun at an address used by Tomek in the *Quartiers Nords* and ballistics have matched that weapon to the death of Juan de Silva in 2007."

"And Delacroix?"

"At the moment he's saying nothing, but the search of his property in Messandrierre has provided some interesting financial information and *Inspecteur* Graves thinks it is just a matter of careful police work to make all the links. He also said that he has requested that the rulings in relation to the suspicious deaths in Canada be re-examined."

Jacques checked his watch. "I need to get back to Beth and Lucien. If you need me for anything for the rest of this week, call me, and I'll come in to catch up two mornings next week. Over to you, Didier."

saturday, september 29th, 11.34

In her studio at the back of the shop, Beth had been sorting through the drawers and shelves and tidying everything. The woman she'd employed to manage the website and shop sales for three mornings a week during her pregnancy, had kept everything more or less up to date. Beth needed to re-stock and she needed everything in exactly the right place before she could determine the extent to which she should re-stock.

"That's much better," she pushed her hair back with the back of her grubby hand. "When I come in next week for a couple of hours I can sort out the orders." She dashed up the narrow stairs to the small kitchen and washed her hands, tidied her hair and left the dusty overall she had been wearing on a hook by the door. As she made her way down her vision became a little blurred and her head felt light for a second or two. She stopped. Her hand on the banister, the knuckles white, she took a couple of deep breaths. The remaining stairs she took more slowly and carefully. She halted again at the bottom step in the studio. Feeling a little clammy, she leaned against the wall for support.

It was three or four minutes later before she felt better. She moved into the shop and sat at the counter for a few more moments and took a long drink from the bottle of water she had brought with her. In her handbag her phone buzzed. She fished it out. A message from Jacques and a picture of Lucien, bright eyed on his mat on the floor. She smiled.

Feeling a little better, Beth collected her keys and bag and locked up at the back. Leaving by the front door, she locked and checked it and set off down the street. A few steps away she returned to check that she really had remembered to lock the door. The sun was warm on her skin as she made her way around the block to where her car was parked.

In the driver's seat she felt dizzy again. Resting her head back and closing her eyes she let the wave of faintness pass.

"I'll be alright in a minute," she assured herself. Remembering she had some mints in a small tin in the glove compartment she got them out and put two in her mouth. The fresh taste revived her and she turned the key. Reversing out she joined the traffic on the main road and threaded her way through the one-way system and out of the city.

The traffic was dense and it was almost twenty minutes before she was climbing up the steep incline towards Badaroux. She glanced at the mountain peaks to her left. The first colours of autumn were beginning to show in the trees and the sun was glinting gold on the leaves.

As she rounded the steep bend coming out of Badaroux she caught a glimpse of Mont Lozère against a deep azure blue sky.

"Lucien, if you could only see that now," she said as she glanced over her shoulder. "Lucien!" She turned and her field of vision went black.

***

In Messandrierre, Jacques was introducing his son to the neighbours as he came across them on his walk around the village. In the bar, Jacques had booked a table for lunch. As he meandered along the road on the edge of the village he encountered Madame Pamier on her way back from the cemetery. She had cooed over the sleeping Lucien and noted how like his father he was.

On the main street, Jacques had stopped off at the Mancelle house. Marie was keeping Pierre at home for a while. Martin had come back from Marseille and had taken leave from his work. Although Pierre was unusually quiet,

Jacques was pleased to see that the family were beginning to put the trauma of the previous week behind them. As he strolled by the church *Père* Chastain appeared and had wondered whether there would be a christening. In the hope of an opportunity to officiate, he had even offered some dates.

Along the top road, Jacques stopped as always and looked over Delacroix's property. The police had undertaken a thorough search, removing his computers and papers and anything else they found of interest.

"With any luck," he said addressing his sleeping son, "Richard Laurent Delacroix won't be back for a long time." The property had been sealed off, the police tape denoting its new significance.

Back in the chalet Jacques, took the carrycot up the spiral staircase to the loft. It was Beth's favourite place to work. From the large full-length windows he could see across the valley to the mountain peaks.

Lucien stirred and Jacques picked him up. "We can see *maman* coming from here," he said. "She'll be back very soon."

As he watched and waited, he saw the small police van that belonged to the village come around the bend and stop outside the chalet. *Gendarme* Thibault Clergue got out. When Jacques saw Clergue come through the small gate, he quickly went down the stairs to meet him at the front door.

"Thibault, I wasn't expecting a visit from you today," he said, his son, wide awake and cradled in his arms.

Thibault straightened his shoulders and took a step back. "Jacques, I'm here as an officer of the law and…and a friend and…I have something very difficult to say. There's been an accident on the steep bends between here and—"

"Beth?" Jacques stood stock still, the tiny child resting against his heart, oblivious.

Thibault nodded, turned his face away and sniffed.

"Are you sure? Is it really Beth?"

It took Thibault a few moments to compose himself. When he finally looked at Jacques, "Yes, I'm sure," he said.

He wiped his finger and thumb across his eyes and stood to attention, hands behind his back as though he was giving evidence in court. "I was first on the scene. The emergency services had already been alerted and arrived eight minutes later. I secured the area. I did everything I could. You need to come with me immediately."

c'est fini

Autumn comes early in the Haute Cévennes to last, seemingly, only a moment before winter strides down from the crest of the corniche. For Jacques, winter had engulfed his heart in its icy grip, the numbing coldness progressing through every thought, memory and emotion. In the early evening darkness of the chalet, he sat immobile as a chill north-easterly sabred through the tiny village of Messandrierre. Hurling gusts of debris at windows, shutters and doors the wind whined its route through crevices and under eaves, seeking a weakness, an opportunity to destroy. Watching the small front gate rocking back and forth to the anger of the wind, Jacques was consumed with a single thought.
How do I come back from this?

glossary of terms

samedi	Saturday
département/s	administrative areas, equivalent to English counties
garde-forestier	forestry official
ma petite, mon petit	my little one – an endearment used between a parent/adult and a child and sometimes an owner and a favourite pet animal
centimes	100 centimes or cents = €1
gendarmerie	rural police station/service
police municipale	local police
maman	mother, mum, mummy
ma chérie, mon cheri	my darling
préfecture	administrative centre for a département
papa	father, dad, daddy
Maire	Mayor
lycée	high/upper school
pain	large loaf of bread
mesdames et messieurs	ladies and gentlemen

Inspecteur principal	Detective Inspector
notaire	lawyer
place	square
rue des Déportés Martyrs	Deported Martyrs' Road
lundi	Monday
Monsieur Souris	Mr Mouse
salon	lounge/living room
ébéniste	cabinetmaker
ferme	farm
bon après-midi	good afternoon
boulevard	street
rue	road
autoroute	motorway
petit	little
Gendarme	policeman
croque monsieur	a toasted ham and cheese sandwich
permis	abbreviation for *permis de conduire*, driving licence
flic	slang for police
route nationale	major road

commune	parish or township
Allo	hello
chemin	way, path or track
avenue	avenue
café	coffee shop
musée des Beaux-Arts	Fine Arts Museum
Vieux Port	Old Port
Quai Neuve	New Bank Quay
pépé	great-grandfather
décor	internal decoration
aperitifs	appetizer
croissant	crescent-shaped pastry
baguette	small loaf
Ça va	greeting equivalent to how are you?
cave	wine cellar
rue des Licornes	Unicorns Road
Les pêcheurs de perles	The Pearl Fishers
Quartiers Nords	Northern Quarters

café allongé	long coffee – an expresso with extra hot water
pression	a draught beer
arrondissement	area of a city, used in Paris and in Marseille, equivalent of Chelsea or Kensington in London
Corniche	coast or ridge of a mountain range
sauvignon blanc	dry white wine made from the sauvignon grape
moules marinières	mussels steamed with garlic, parsley, butter and white wine
frites	fries
pains au chocolat	pastry with a chocolate centre
Fermier	farmer
la réserve	inheritance rites of children and other family members
disparu	disappeared
n = née	born
concierge	apartment building caretaker
charcuterie	cooked and prepared meats
Pélardon	small round cheese made from raw goats milk, although widely available it originates from the Cévennes
Bonjour	good morning

matrice cadastrale	the equivalent of Land Registry records in the UK
accidentel	accidental
Père	Father, when addressing a priest
c'est fini	it ends

Fantastic Books
Great Authors

darkstroke is
an imprint of
Crooked Cat Books

- Gripping Thrillers
- Cosy Mysteries
- Romantic Chick-Lit
- Fascinating Historicals
- Exciting Fantasy
- Young Adult and Children's Adventures
- Non-Fiction

Discover us online
www.darkstroke.com

Find us on instagram:
www.instagram.com/darkstrokebooks

Printed in Great Britain
by Amazon